My Daughter's Eyes
and Other Stories

ANNECY BÁEZ

Curbstone Press

Printed on acid-free paper in the U.S.

Cover design and photograph: Susan Shapiro

Connecticut Commission
on Culture & Tourism

This book was published with the support of the
Connecticut Commission on Culture and Tourism, The
Connecticut State Legislature through the Office Of
Policy and Management, and donations from many individuals.
We are very grateful for this support.

Library of Congress Cataloging-in-Publication Data

Baez, Annecy.
    My daughter's eyes, and other stories / by Annecy Baez.
      p. cm.
    ISBN-13: 978-1-931896-38-2 (pbk. : alk. paper)
    ISBN-10: 1-931896-38-0 (pbk. : alk. paper)
    1. Dominican Americans—New York (State)—New York—Social life and
customs—Fiction. 2. Immigrants—Fiction. I. Title.

    PS3602.A385M93 2007
    813'.6—dc22

                                        2006028832

published by
    CURBSTONE PRESS   321 Jackson Street   Willimantic, CT 06226
          phone: 860-423-5110   e-mail: info@curbstone.org
                    http://www.curbstone.org

*"There are a lot of shoulds
that happen in this world,
which means there are a lot
of things
that happen
that shouldn't have..."*

from
The Adventures of Pinocchio
Carlo Collodi

CONTENTS

Para
Mami y Papi
Missing your presence here on earth

My Daughter's Eyes and Other Stories

The Storyteller
2000

In the morning when the sun rises, my mother, Mia, wakes up and does her morning meditation. She always does this before she goes to work. I always know for a fact that by 6:30 a.m., she will be facing east towards the sun, her face covered by sunlight. She'll be in lotus pose, legs folded like a Buddha, hands open with her palms facing the ceiling, and both placed neatly, the left on top of the right. She always faces east, and she takes in the rays of the sun because they are healing, she says.

I feel fortunate with my life, with the structure she provides, knowing that every morning when I wake up she will be there doing her meditation and that I will take a bath and get dressed and have breakfast with her, and later I will come home, and she will be returning from work always at the same time. Sometimes, in the evening when she does her meditation, I will sit with her for five minutes and then when my legs have had enough, and the fantasies in my head begin to feel real, like I'm getting married to Usher and he writes songs about me, it's time to go, and I slowly get up and leave. My mom says that a person becomes disciplined by taking baby steps. You do a small thing and in time that becomes a big thing. At times she makes me feel that there is nothing to fear and that life is good, beautiful and it makes me want to tell stories.

I watch her now; I have her Maybeline eyeliner in my hands, and I will ask her to do my eyes. I want them just like Jennifer Lopez, but I know she'll put up a fight and say that I am too young, thirteen to be exact, and she'll remind me of some time in the past when she was thirteen, and she'll go on and on. Often I wonder if in those meditative moments she can really remember the past, back then when I was not born yet, and she was about my age and thinking of boys.

There are days when she tells me stories. Even when I

1

was a little girl she'd tell me stories while she cooked or drove, stories about her life. Some stories she told openly, honestly; others she hid from me. I would have to decipher her silences like a puzzle, or a riddle. Sometimes, when she tells me stories, I listen and record them in my mind, and those that she does not share, I invent.

Amor Sucks

Wednesday, January 12, 1972
Bronx, New York
"Hump Day"

Cousin Eva and our best friend America lock themselves in the bedroom with the boys. They usually start slowly. Eva goes with Snake and then Rica follows, then Pito. I stay alone in the sunken living room, hearing the Temptations or watching "One Life to Live." Sometimes it is quiet here and I can listen to the noises they make and the giggles. Today, Pito stays with me watching "One Life to Live," until he hears the sounds coming from his father's bedroom, the ohh, ahh, ahh, and the laughter calling out to him like spices.

He says "You want to come?" and I say "Na, I'm not ready for that," and catch myself worrying that Pito will think I'm not tough enough to be a Dragon Slayer. Pito and his brother, Snake, are the leaders of the Dragon Slayers, and so being with them makes us Slayer girls. Kind of.

The Dragon Slayers wear black leather jackets with a red and yellow dragon on the back, and multicolored letters drawn on the bottom that say "Dragon Slayer." We're not officially Dragon Slayer girls until we wear our jackets with our pants. But at the moment, we're not allowed to wear pants, and the jackets don't look cool with our dresses. I wear mini dresses, but Eva's religious father, Tío Quinto, forbids her to wear them. Eva wears colorless clothes, black knee-high skirts and white blouses, like she's going to church. She looks like a saint, but she doesn't fool anyone at Wade Junior High because Eva is tough and beautiful. Today, she wore Snake's jacket over her long black skirt and no one dared to mess with her because she's a Dragon Slayer. Someday I'll wear Pito's jacket, and I'll feel beautiful, strong, and cool, too.

3

Snake and Pito are twins, but I can tell them apart because Snake is mean and willful, just like Eva. He likes to grab and touch what doesn't belong to him; he's hard like an old callus. Pito is sweet and won't try anything unless he thinks you want him to. He's calm and gentle when he's alone with me, but when he's with Snake he acts just like him, mean and tough.

Pito wears a whistle around his neck. That's why they call him Pito. He tells me his mother bought him the whistle when he was just five years old. Shortly after that she died of cancer. He wears the whistle proudly. It's his protection, he says, and a memory of his mother. He won't let anyone touch that damn whistle.

Now Pito stares at me, and gives me his hand.

"You don't want to come?" he asks, and I just stay quiet, wondering what to say next. My hands start to shake as he comes close to me, and I hide them underneath my skinny thighs, but they still tremble like the trees on the Grand Concourse on a stormy night. He kneels in front of me, and I steady myself with a deep breath.

"I don't know," I say, because I'm not sure I'm ready for the kissing and touching stuff they are doing to each other in the bedroom. I could act like I know, like I'm ready, and be scared in there, or I can say I'm not ready and not play hooky with them anymore, except that I don't have the guts because I want to belong. I want to be loved, and to be part of something big, something like the Dragon Slayers.

Pito sits next to me on the sofa. I sit like a good girl with my hands on my lap. My thighs sweat and stick to the plastic of the mustard colored sofa, and I don't dare look at him as he comes close to me. I look at my folded hands and move my face away when he tries to kiss me. He stops and stands up.

"You don't want to come?" he asks.

I look at him closely. He's standing in front of me, and I realize I want to go wherever he wants me to go because I like him, but I'm not ready for that. My heart starts pounding and I can see my chest rising. Pito is beautiful and I want to please him. But I don't want him to think I'm so easy like a puppy who will "sit" or "stand". I have to give myself *importancia,* a sense of importance, and then I give in, according to Eva. Eva knows everything.

I look Pito up and down. He's tall, and dark-skinned with long, brown, curly hair, soft to the touch. His lips are always wet and smooth, reminding me of a ripe juicy mango. I'm quiet, and don't know what to say to him. I've never liked a boy this much. I've never had a boy as cute as Pito want me and just because of this I feel my heart swell. I feel so important and special, different from everyone else.

Pito stares at me now, waiting for my response.

I say, "What?"

"Do you want to come to the room?" He shakes his head a little towards the direction of his father's bedroom. He's sitting next to me now. He leans toward me and gives me a kiss. This is not one of our usual, little pecking kisses, but long, his tongue twirling and locking with mine. I taste Juicy Fruit gum and a hint of his musk oil. I want to eat him.

I return his deep wide kiss as if I know how to do this with a boy. I kiss him like I see people kiss on "One Life to Live," only better. His kisses release something new inside of me, like a butterfly flying inside of my stomach. Deep within me this new feeling takes wings. I want to fly. I don't know what to do with these feelings because something is happening to my *pompo* private part as he's kissing me, a new sensation, and slight flutter, something moving about down there as if my palpitating heart just sank there like an anchor. I feel like I have to pee. Then thoughts of Papi come to mind. A warning. I push Pito away. Full of shame, I take a deep breath. I don't know what to say to him.

But, God, a part of me wishes I could just run into that bedroom with him because there's this new feeling inside of me. I want to kiss like this for a long time, and float on the riverbed of his father's room, letting him hold me and play with me. Pito stands up and says, "Come!" as he gives me his hand. "Na, you go," I say "because I'm not ready," and he goes and that's okay.

Saturday, January 29, 1972
Day of New Beginnings

"Are you coming?" Eva asks me. It's late at night and I'm lying on my back staring at the ceiling in Eva's bedroom. Eva is next to me, staring at me and asking endless questions. I like to stay over on the weekend. Our whole family lives in the same building on 170th street in the Bronx, one on top of each other, like steps on a ladder, my grandmother, *la Guela*, *los Tíos* and *las Tías*, and a whole bunch of cousins.

I stare at her. "Coming?" I ask. I take a deep sigh and I can smell the coconut oil of her hair, the cool peppermint scent of her mouth, and see the sparkles of talcum powder left on her breast, now exposed through her thin nightgown.

Eva is so pretty with her light smooth skin like sea stones and eyes a blue violet set upon her heart-shaped Dominican face. Her dark hair is chin length and kinky like Brillo, *pelo malo*, "bad hair" the family calls it, but Eva doesn't go around envying the straight more silkier hair of her cousins because at fourteen she looks eighteen and her huge breasts are a source of pride to her. Often, she measures them with the hope that they continue their promising course. Me. I'm odd. I don't have the almond shaped light eyes of the women in my family, or their heart shaped face with the pointy little chin, and the straight, small nose. No, I have a wide nose like sighing mountains across my face, and large thick lips Papi calls a *"bembe"*. *"Y ese bembe, Mia?"* he'll question whenever I pout. *Bembe*, lips, big lips, lips so big I often try to hide them by pressing them against each other in a thin line. And I don't have Eva's eyes, I have small Asian dark eyes like my paternal grandfather El Chino, and I'm skinny and tall, not the kind of girl the cute Dominican boys in the corner *colmado* say things to like "*Mami tú si 'ta buena*" and stuff like that, the kind of stuff they tell Eva when she passes by them.

Eva awakens me from my thoughts.

"Mia, are you coming?"

"Where?"

"To Pito's, idiot."

"Oh, Pito's."

It's been two weeks since I've seen Pito in his apartment. I see him in school, in the hallways fooling around with the girls, pulling their hair or talking to them softly. I won't speak to him for hours afterwards.

When I stay with Eva we often talk about the boys and plan our whole week at Wade Junior High School. Before the boys, we used to skip school, go to Alexander's on Fordham Road, and look at clothing. Sometimes we'd sneak in the white people's buildings on the Concourse. We'd sit on the pretty sofas in their building entrances, or maybe take the elevator up and down until one of the old women with blue tattooed numbers on her wrist asked us to leave or threatened to call the police.

Lately I've been thinking it's dangerous to go to the Pito's apartment. I can have babies now because blood flows through my legs once a month. My Godmother, Tati, says that these bad feelings are *presentimientos*, and when you have a *presentimiento* she says it's your inner voice telling you to be careful. She says women have a strong inner voice. Lately I don't listen to my inner voice.

"I don't know, Eva," I say to her and she jumps up.

"What?"

"I said I don't know. I think we'll get caught."

" Are you getting chickenshit on me?" she asks.

"No."

7

"Oh, ok," she says, "so that means you're coming, right?"

"I guess so."

We lie on the bed, and she is on her side looking at me.

"You're not going to change your mind?"

"No."

"Cause Pito's expecting you," she says. "You know?"

"Really?" I ask because I want to hear it again.

"Yeah, he's been asking like crazy about you."

I smile, and the thought of Pito wanting me there makes me feel warm all over, and my heart swells at the thought of him. I turn on my side and stare at her, our faces up close.

"I'm coming," I say, and she smiles.

Thursday, February 22, 1972
Amor Sucks

I'm getting scared of playing hooky because I'm kissing Pito more times than I probably should. I know Eva and Rica are doing sex stuff with Snake in the bedroom, but I act like I don't know. Now Pito and I have kissing marathons, long kisses without breathing, sucking kisses; light nibbling kisses and dry kisses that leave our lips chapped and tired, and these kisses are so powerful they make us want to do more than just kiss.

Now Pito won't go with Eva and Rica in the bedroom but wants to stay with me in the living room. He says I'm beautiful, more beautiful than Eva and Rica. He says I'm smart too and that he likes that. He says I'm his special girl. I'm scared because I really like him and when you really like a boy you want to do everything with him. You want to share the world with him.

Now my inner voice is whispering Shh, shh, shh.

I don't listen to it anymore, that inner voice inside that warns me of danger all the time. I don't. I listen to my body which reminds me of the fun things I'll experience when

Pito's soft lips suck on my lips or his hands touch me, leaving his memory all over my body.

I don't listen to that voice even when kids in school tell me Pito does this stuff with other girls or when ex-Dragon Slayer girls remind me that they were in my place just a month or two ago, and out of the blue, Pito dumped them. I don't listen to them. I ignore the lies and gossip of has-beens. I only listen to my heart. Maybe those rumors are true, but Pito has a special place for me in his heart. I'm different from other girls, I remind myself. I'm special. Lately, I've been feeling very, very special, but Rica says this is trouble. She says you have to be real cool with a boy, not take him too serious, and expect that he might leave. She says boys are like dogs and the next thing you know they need a brand new bone to bone, and I laugh, but what she means is that one day, out of the blue, Pito could be gone, gone with some other girl, gone like the wind with no cause or reason.

That happened to Rica when she was with Romero. All she did was feel special and then he left her for Julieta. And what did we see? Hearts all over the handball courts, on walls, halls and in the bathroom. Hearts that said Romero and Julieta 1972 forever. Bilingual hearts in Spanish that said *"Amor Para Siempre,"* Love forever, Romero y Julieta, and Cupid's arrow inside of the heart connecting them until death separated them. Rica was devastated, but it didn't last long, because Eva wouldn't let her feel sorry for herself. She said boys were like lollipops, they came in different flavors and sizes, and there were too many of them to cry over the loss of one, so over the hearts for Romero and Julieta they drew hearts, large hearts with daggers, dripping blood and in between them they wrote *"Amor Sucks."*

Saturday, March 4, 1972
Day of Resolution

La Negra, my old cloth doll from Santo Domingo, and I are
sleeping over at Eva's tonight. It's a dark night and the moon
is full. The wind whistles loudly outside, banging at our
window like a warning.

I tell Eva I can't do it anymore.

"Just once more," she says, "Mia, please!"

"Ok, Eva, but we promise, after this no more playing
hooky, ok," I say, but I don't look convinced, and Eva says
"Scouts Honor," and that makes me laugh because we are
not Girl Scouts. Our family is too strict for that. They don't
allow us to participate in any group activities, to visit the
homes of other kids or to have friends other than our cousins
play with us. We're not even allowed to go on school trips
and Papi and Mami, they've never even been to Wade Junior
High. I wish they would, just for one day so they could feel
the danger.

Just the other day, the Javelins plotted to take Shakela's
wig off. She's a big, bald, black girl who wears a wig. When
they took off her wig, we saw her bald head. She started to
scream this wailing sound so painful I can still hear it in my
head. "Mama, Mama, Mama" she screamed as if she were
dying, "Mama, Mama, Mama" and she threw herself on the
floor, crying, so humiliated by her exposure, "Mama, Mama,
Mama," she cried and no one dared to go to her until Ms.
Will, the gym teacher who looks like a man, came and took
her to the infirmary. Shakela's wig dangling from the
handball court fence was left behind like a defeated flag.

Papi is still under the erroneous belief that school in the
Bronx is a safe place and that we are being taught the lessons
of the day. He doesn't know that the books are old, torn and
in poor condition. He doesn't know that for the most part we
are too scared to learn. So one day I said to Papi, "Things
have to change around here because the world out there is

not the world of this family." That was the beginning of the end, Papi slammed his fist on the table, breaking a plate, and gave me one of his dirty looks, and I felt as if he'd smacked me. I know never to remind him that in Junior High I live in one world and at home I live in another. I'm safer with Pito, though. No one messes with me because I'm a Dragon Slayer, and I have the colors to prove it, too. So Eva is asking me about playing hooky, and I weigh what I will do in school with what I will do with the boys, and the boys are winning out, although I know it's wrong and I can get pregnant and I can shame my family.

"We won't get caught," Eva says.

"We'll stop, right?"

"Dragon Slayer's honor," she says and we laugh.

The heater hisses like a train, and the room is unbearably hot. Eva suggests we take our nightgowns off, and we do, and I can feel her large, sweaty breasts brush against my arm. She makes fun of the largeness of my nipples, and I make fun of the fact that she has huge breasts with tiny nipples like dots at the end of a sentence.

"You won't be able to breast-feed," I tell her.

"There are other things better than breast feeding," she says and leaves me wondering, but I guess I know what she means.

We lay in bed, and we're uncomfortable, unable to find a good sleeping position in her twin bed. We decide to curl up like spoons, and Eva hugs me tight, as she tends to do. I can feel her hand caressing me, soft circles around my back, up and down motions, sliding towards the front, on my stomach now, and I begin to feel those feelings I'm not ready for, and I say "pinky promise," and give her my pinky. "No more hooky playing,"

"Pinky promise," she says, and we cuddle together in the night, Eva sucking on her thumb until she falls asleep and me holding on to La Negra, my favorite doll Papi bought me

11

from Santo Domingo. Even now, she smells like vanilla milk and cinnamon sticks. I hold her tight by my side.

Wednesday, Hump Day
Last Day of Hooky Playing
March 8, 1972

Eva and Rica lock themselves in the bedroom with Snake, and they want Pito and me to join them. They remind us that the bed is a waterbed, and I say "five's a crowd," and Pito says, "Yeah, five's a crowd." Pito and I stay in the living room and he starts to kiss me as soon as the door closes. We hear the waterbed rolling like an ocean. He kisses me in that special kind of way that leaves me open. He starts to touch me, as his mouth is wide open on my mouth. I don't wear a bra because Mami won't let me. A bra will give me ideas that I'm a woman, she says, even though you can see my breasts, and I can have babies now. Parents have crazy ideas, and Mami, she's crazy like that sometimes. Now, I can feel the warmth of Pito's hands through my dress. I feel strange new sensations all over my body that scare me and so my heart is beating fast, and my breathing is so deep I can hear it.

"You are the best kisser," Pito says to me, and I laugh, but my laughter ends when he says, "Better than Eva, and Rica, and better than any of the girls at Wade Junior High," and I don't know if to be proud or mad, I let it go because I'm feeling good, so soft like a fluffy cloud. "Yes," he says, "So good," and he says it with so much feeling, the good lingering in my ear, and I feel so proud to be wanted by him, to be cared by him, to be thought of as special.

"You are such a special girl, my special girl," he says, and I feel like I've won some love competition against a whole bunch of girls I haven't even met. I'm feeling special too, so special that I let his hand touch my thigh, his hand is warm and soft like velvet, and it goes up and down in a soft caress, and his touch brings up new feelings on my thigh, feelings I had not felt before.

I'm not allowed to wear pants to school because I am a girl and my parents feel that a girl should not wear pants, so I walk around with just short mini dresses with buttons in the front, and knee high socks, like a child. He holds me and I feel great, better than I have felt before, I'm silly putty in his arms. I start to laugh at my own thoughts. I feel his breath on my cheeks. His tongue traces the faint veins on my neck while he holds me tight. I feel warm. He kisses my neck, making me feel a tingle down my spine, and he says, "Relax," and I do. He kisses my cheeks again. I open my mouth waiting for him. He kisses me, and I breathe him in deeply. He stops and then he murmurs in between kisses, "You want to blow my whistle?"

This request surprises me. Pito wears his whistle around his neck; there it dangles on an old brown suede cord like a medal, a memory of his dead mother, and I'm surprised at his request because no one touches Pito's whistle. So I touch it, and it's soft, warm from the heat of his body and I start to hold it and Pito laughs and he smacks my hand, "Not that whistle, silly," and he takes my right hand and puts it on top of his pants where his zipper has been open for some time. It's warm, hard and lumpy there where he places my hand, and I'm surprised because I wouldn't know how to blow that whistle at all. Now, my joy and pleasure in being with Pito is replaced by a feeling of fear; a terror goes through my body as if I've been caught in a lie and so I say, "No thanks."

"It would make me very happy," he says, and I know it would, but I can't. I would only blow the metal whistle around his neck, and he says "No one touches that whistle" and he holds it. I smile and suddenly decide that I will be the first to blow on Pito's whistle, the metal whistle that dangles from his neck, a memory of his dead mother. I will be the one to touch it without having to do anything I am not ready to do with him, and so I kiss his lips softly, sweetly and then kiss his eyes and his ears. He relaxes in my arms and so I kiss his neck breathing in the scent of his musk oil. I kiss him slowly on his chest where the metal whistle is waiting for me. He lets go of it and his hands caress my back while I give him small little baby kisses on his chest until I reach his metal whistle, and kiss it slowly; I look at him and kiss the metal whistle again. He lets me.

I look at him slowly, and put the metal whistle ever so gently inside of my mouth, and he lets me do that too. I blow it and it whistles, a low, silly whistle and it makes him laugh and now I feel really special because no one I know at Wade Junior High has put Pito's whistle in her mouth and has blown on it. Now, my tongue is all over Pito's whistle. The metal is warm. Then Pito kisses me gently on the mouth, me with the whistle in my mouth and we kiss there, Pito, the whistle and me. I open my eyes as he kisses me and I stare at him, his eyes are dark and his lashes long, he opens his eyes and looks at me. Eva says it's bad luck to open your eyes when you're kissing, but there we are kissing with our eyes wide open.

Pito pauses and says, "I'm going to leave you a little gift, a love bite," and I nod yes and he says "a love bruise, something to remember me by," and he sucks real hard on my neck like a vampire while I giggle, but then as I relax I start to feel this little rush like a flutter of butterflies inside my body and this feeling takes over like a shudder so delicious that I let go and just lie there on the sofa. It is good and new, this feeling. Nothing like what I feel when I practice kissing with Rica, nothing like what I feel when I touch myself. This is new, different and a rush comes over me so strong that my body moves to the rhythm of his touch, and his kisses and all that sucking creates feeling down inside of me that I have never felt before. It is such a happy feeling that I feel connected to all that there is in the world. I start to think of God, *la Virgencita de la Altagracia,* and even of baby Jesus, and I feel so close to God, closer than I've ever been. I start to cry, saying "Oh, God, God," and my body can't take it, and then I'm trembling in his arms, and he is laughing and kissing my lips and my eyes.

I wonder what my parents would think of me if they found out. What would Papi say if he knew his thirteen year old daughter was out with a boy in his apartment, letting him touch her and liking it? I see Papi's angry face, and I see Mami, crying in the palm of her hands. I think of Ms. Rodriguez, my homeroom teacher, who said we should never play hooky with the boys. I think of Mrs. White, my typing teacher, with her shriveled face and her hunched back reminding me that I need to learn to type, it's the only way to get a job. I hear her screaming at me because I've missed her class. Maybe she called my parents. Suddenly, all these faces loom over me, my father, mother, grandmother, my teachers, pointing their fingers at me, disappointed with me, and I feel great shame.

Pito comes towards me for a kiss. I push him away.

I feel nauseous. I feel dizzy.

"I can have babies now," I say repeatedly and he starts to laugh.

"Not like this, Mia," he says. "Not like this. We haven't had sex."

I am speechless when he uses the S word.

"I love you," he says with all of this sweetness, and I am disgusted. "You make me so happy," he adds and he comes close to me, and I want him to move away, so I push him away. My hands are trembling as I button my blouse. I am confused. I don't understand all of my feelings, and I start to cry because no boy has told me he loves me, not like Pito, not like that. No boy has touched me and made me tremble in his arms. I button my blouse, and tears begin to fall down my cheeks onto my lap. I am confused.

"Why are you crying?" he asks and comes to soothe me, but his need for me turns my stomach.

"Leave me alone," I say to him, and he moves away with a hurt look, his eyes growing misty with tears.

I'm glad this will be the last time I play hooky, I say to myself, because I don't know what I'm doing and a part of me can't stop. I get taken over by these feelings that are too strong for me to understand and I'm lost, so lost.

And what about all of these feelings in my body? Is this love? Yes, it has to be love I say to myself. I must love him too, or I wouldn't be feeling these feelings, but I want to throw up. I'm disgusted with the whole thing, and I can't say "I love you" back to him. I just can't. I get up nervously. I ignore him when he tries to hold my arm. I go towards his father's bedroom and I knock on the door. I tell Eva it's time to leave. I can smell the sweet smoke coming from in there, mixed with Jasmine incense and I can hear the Temptations real low on the radio.

"Let's go, Eva," I say to her as I knock.

I hear the waterbed rolling, making wave sounds as they move on it.

"I'm coming, I'm coming," I hear Eva whispering and Rica's little laughter.

"Eva, Eva, let's go," I say.

"Yeeeesss, yes..." I hear her say "I...I...I'm coming."

"Ok, Ok, I'll wait," I say, and so I wait.

The Red Shoes

The warm, humid air was still when Zuleika and her mother, Tati, arrived at the Mejia Shoe Store on 181 Street and Saint Nicholas Avenue. Zuleika sensed a calm promise of excitement in the air, the kind that is in the air when one is young and full of joy.

"I like these shoes for you, Zuki," her mother said in her accented English as she pointed at the window display. Zuleika stared at the black, flat, leather shoes her mother was admiring. They were the ugliest pair of shoes she had ever seen.

"*Ay*, Mami, *por favor*, that's for a *jamona*," Zuleika said, quickly regretting her irreverence, but feeling quite secure that her perception was accurate. Those flat ugly shoes were for an old maid. Who in their right mind would look at a girl wearing them?

"*Deja de contestarme asi*, Zuleika, *por favor*," her mother said in her stern Dominican intonation as she glanced at Zuleika up and down and rolled her eyes.

"I'm sorry, Mami," Zuleika responded, avoiding her mother's eyes as she fanned herself with a copy of a *Seventeen* magazine she was holding.

"*¿Pero es que tú ya no me respetes, muchacha?*" Tati questioned.

"I respect you. I do. I didn't mean to answer back. Sorry, Mami, sorry!" she said as she continued looking at the black flats in the window display, and mustering some feigned interest in them.

"The black shoes are kind of cute, Má, but..."

"But, what? What's the problem? *¿No, están de moda?*" Tati asked with curiosity in her eyes.

"No, Má, no, they're not in style," Zuleika responded flatly.

"Ok, Zuki, Ok," Tati said as she inhaled some warm air and exhaled her impatience.

The mid-day sun grew brighter and the humidity rose. Tati was hot and uncomfortable as she took a deep breath and quietly browsed the window display. As she looked at all the pretty shoes, her thoughts turned to Julio, her young lover. He had been her professor at Lehman College where she taken Advanced English in the Continuing Education Program. Now, Julio was her lover.

Ay Julio, Tati sighed in her thoughts, thinking about how in his arms she fulfilled yearnings, so pleasurable, they felt like sins. Suddenly, her heart raced fast and skipped beats as thoughts and images of her sexual escapades lingered through her mind. A sudden hotness seemed to overtake her, and she touched her chest with the palm of her hand. She took a deep breath. She hated these dreadful feelings. She hated them. *Cálmate* she said to herself. Calm down, she repeated.

Tati moved closer to Zuleika and found some peace in her presence. Her daughter had grown tall and beautiful, but she could not find words to share this with her. In a few weeks Zuleika would turn fifteen. God, where had the years gone by she thought? Zuleika was a *Señorita* in her own right, but with her upcoming birthday came a certain feeling of loss and solitude as if a long chapter of Tati's life had ended and a new one was beginning. She stared at Zuleika's young shoulders and felt a desire to hold her like when she was small, maybe to find comfort in her arms for the fear she could not understand. As Tati walked closer to her, she noticed that the ugliest pair of red shoes had mesmerized Zuleika. Red shoes were certainly not appropriate for a young decent Dominican girl, Tati thought.

Zuleika stood in front of the window display, staring at the most beautiful red shoes she had ever seen. Her eyes remained fixed until she was surprised by her own skinny image reflecting on the window display. She was tall for her age, she thought, a bit too skinny, and she viewed with shame the skinny legs she would thicken with three pairs of stockings whenever she wore a dress or a skirt.

Her friends had nice big breasts, thick thighs, curvaceous hips and *nalgas* that left the young men in distress when they walked by. The men said things like "*Mami chula, tú si está buena,*" as they licked their lips, but all they said to her was "*Flaca, mira flaca.*" Those reference to her thinness would pierce her heart, shatter her in some unexpected way. She didn't want to be a *flaca*, a skinny little thing. She wanted to be fuller, that was it, so men would say "*pero Mami, tú si está buena.*" This wish she kept a secret to herself.

The truth was that she ate, *Arroz con pollo*, rice and beans with stewed tongue, fried green plantain, but no, her body refused to grow into the voluptuous proportions so admired by Latin men. Men. God, she wished that their approval did not mean so much to her.

As she moved back to find something in herself that pleased her, her focus returned once again to the pair of red shoes. The red shoes stood motionless, and discreetly tucked in the top right of the window display. Every shoe on the display had a name, "Rosaura", "Amayra", and "Yadira". Her red shoes were called simply "Celestina". Yes, Celestina was a right name for her pretty shoes. They were a simple pair of proud pumps; with four-inch heels and high arch and Oh God they were so beautiful. Inside of those pretty shoes, she would be stunning. Yes, she would. Those proud pumps would lift her butt and thicken her calves, and people would admire her. She saw herself walking in them and the boys staring at her and saying "*Mami, qué zapato más lindo,* but more than that they would say "*Mami, pero tú si ta' buena.*"

As Zuleika continued staring at her wonderful shoes, she managed to see the beautiful image of her mother looking right through her with the kind of glistening in her eyes that often told Zuleika that her mother was out to spoil her fun.

But then she noticed that even further beyond the mirage of her mother's eyes, past the shoes on the display and inside of the store was a brown man with the bluest eyes and he stared at her and smiled. He was older, not as old as her mother was, but almost there. He seemed rich, sophisticated and composed, and somehow familiar even though he was a stranger. Zuleika felt a sudden surge of heat go all through her body. A sense of panic overtook her. She lowered her eyes and quickly moved towards her mother, finding solace in her presence. She held on to her mother's arm, and they walked into the store.

Tati noticed how Zuleika scurried quickly to her side and found comfort in her arms. Tati smiled. She was glad that Zuleika had come to her senses and was behaving more like the little girl she once knew, but as they entered the store, Tati could not help but notice the handsome brown man with the blue eyes who stared at them. Whose beauty was he admiring? She wondered.

The Mejia shoe store was noisy, crowded and freezing. The old brown rug was water-stained and musty from the oversized, leaking air conditioner mounted above the entrance. The voices of the young echoed as loudly as the music on the radio. A powerful, deep voice aggressively promised sex and other pleasures to the beat of drums and congas. The oozing scent of bubble gum and perfume came out of the excited adolescent girls looking for promises of love in a pair of shoes.

A young Dominican salesman with an Arab face and a long ponytail approached Zuleika, who quickly ordered her shoes without her mother noticing.

"*Celestina, por favor*, size *seis* or six and a half. I'll try both," she said in a polite whisper. As she waited, Zuleika noticed that her hands were sweaty. She feared one of her mother's unforgiving public displays, her sudden outburst of verbal abuse.

While Zuleika waited for her shoes, Tati was lost in thought. She stared at all of the shoes. Shoes...shoes.... shoes... Tati thought, as memories of Julio, her lover, re-surfaced like an illicit dream. "*Mami, ven, ven, así, sí, así,*" he said to her as they made love. She thought about the strengths of his desire and her weakness. She felt exposed and vulnerable, aroused by his youth and masculinity. She was so ashamed to have succumbed to him without resistance. "*Ay, sí, sí, así,*" she said to him without realizing that she had said that. *Ay, Dios* she thought, wishing the memories away.

Julio would buy her shoes, patent leather stilettos that Tati would wear with sexy lingerie. Mostly the sexy attire reminded her that she was no longer young, but to Julio she was beautiful at forty-five and in his arms she found herself anew, again and again. He was so strong, and hard, and oh God, how he exploded inside her as she lost control, scratching and biting him. *Ay, Dios.*

But, she was wrong. It was wrong to make love to Julio on the anniversary of her husband's death. It had been ten years now, but still, she should have shown respect for the dead. However, on that anniversary night, wearing her red lingerie with her matching heels, Tati clung to Julio like a vine, and she wept when he penetrated parts of her body and mind that had not been reached in a long time. Such vanity and selfishness, she thought, such disrespect for the dead.

Tati felt her face flush. She touched her forehead. She was hot and sweaty again, and she wasn't feeling well, yet it was exceedingly cool in the store. Tati was suddenly startled out of her thoughts by the gentle and cheerful voice of the young salesman.

"*Señorita,* you have here "*Celestina,*" our popular new model imported directly from Spain," the young salesman said.

"*Gracias*," Zuleika said as she carefully took one shoe out of the box, holding it like an ancient flute made of bones and glass. Her thoughts lingered in slow motion as she fantasized that the shoes were made of flesh, long, hard and palpitating in her hand like a man's delicate penis, imploring to be held, touched and blessed, but her mother's fury was more than she expected, and she felt the impact of her mother's rage.

"What the hell do you think you are doing, Zuleika?" her mother said, snatching the shoe from her hand.

Zuleika was too numb to speak. Her soul ached at the sight of her delicate red shoes in her mother's grasp.

"Let them go, Mami, *tú dijiste*..."

"*Yo no dije nada, carajo!* Zuleika"

"You said that on my fifteen birthday..."

"No, no, no. *Nada de* fifteen birthday. You are not going out like a *quero* in those shoes," her mother said. "Only whores wear those shoes. Look at this heel. *Que tú te' cree*, Zuleika?"

"*Pero, Mami*," Zuleika managed to say.

"No, no, no. *Carajo!*" Tati whispered in a hoarse, insistent voice, like someone possessed by an evil spirit. "Where in the hell do you think you are going to go with those red shoes?"

"But Mami, what's wrong with them? They're beautiful."

"They're too high." Tati said "and too red," she added and suddenly her thought flashed to memories of her in bed with Julio again. She recalled his tender voice saying "*High. Put your leg up higher. Asi si. Your legs. Si. Tati, come honey, come. Come to me.*" Tati's hands trembled. She wanted the intrusive thoughts to go away, for his voice in her mind to go away.

Zuleika noticed the sudden flush on her mother's cheeks, but she thought nothing of it as she pressed her appeal.

"Why, Mami, why?"

"They're too high, Zuki."

"High?"

"Yes, they're too high for you. You could hurt your ovaries.

"*Diablo*, Má. How do you come up with these things?" Zuleika asked.

"*Los ovarios son delicados*, Zuleika, and ... you're just developing them. Do you want to ruin them forever?"

"Ovaries, ovaries, *Ay, Mami por favor*. My friends wear pretty shoes like these by their fifteen birthday and they don't hurt their ovaries."

Tati looked at the red shoes one more time, trying to imagine her young daughter in them, but no, they were too sexy. Too high. Too red. She pursed her lips and shook her head from side to side, rejecting Zuleika's appeal.

"They're too red," Tati affirmed.

"Red, Mami, they are red shoes," Zuleika answered tersely, wanting desperately to penetrate her foot into them, to feel their soft cushion inside, and to rise above it all.

"No, no," Tati continued, as she reflected once again on Julio's preferences, and the thought made her flush and sweat. In her mind she heard him saying, "*Honey, red, red, looks so good on you... it heightens the caramelo color of your skin, ven conmigo Mami, ven mi caramelo, come let me...let me...*" She closed her eyes, hoping that with this simple gesture of temporary blindness the thoughts would disappear.

Re-opening her eyes, she turned to her daughter. "No, Zuleika, *ya está bueno*, no red shoes," she said. "No Celestinas for you."

"Why, Mami. Please," Zuleika implored, begging her mother for another variation of "no."

"Zuki, if I let you wear those shoes, it'll be the end. I can just imagine it. Soon you'll be in bed with some nasty Dominican man all over you...and then the next thing we know you're pregnant at fifteen. I'm not raising a grandchild ...no way."

"*Diantre*, Mami, I'm already pregnant and I haven't worn these shoes," Zuleika said as she looked at the red shoes squirming out of her mother's hand, gasping for air and wishing for life. "Pregnant, who ever heard of such a thing?" she added defiantly.

"*Coño*, Zuleika Altagracia, *por favor es qué tú no entiendes. Respetame, carajo*!!" Tati said, her patience evaporated, and not caring that everyone was noticing their argument. "*¿Tú quiere que te de galleta?*" She threatened.

Zuleika looked around her. No, she did not want to get smacked in front of all of these people, but shit, man; she wasn't any eight-year-old anymore. She was almost fifteen.

"Mami, give me the shoes," Zuleika said tersely, abandoning the sweet-ass approach in favor of an icy directive.

"No," Tati repeated.

"Mami, they're just a pair of shoes," Zuleika said, suffering for their fate, strangled as they were in her mother's grip.

"So what, you're not wearing them," her mother responded. "To be in the street like some slut, no."

"Why do you always relate things to sex? Zuleika questioned. "You have sex on your mind a lot more than I do," she added.

The coldness in Zuleika's tone made Tati feel momentarily alone. But the distance was quickly bridged by her swelling anger. "*Mire, Carajo,* don't you dare... talk to me this way," she spurted furiously as people stared once again. "Have you loss your senses, Zuleika. How dare you answer back and talk to me like a peer about sex. How dare you, Zuleika. Apologize, this instant," Tati said, spitting fire with every word.

"I'm sorry, Mami, I'm sorry," Zuleika cried in a childish voice. "Just give me a break."

"No, break *del carajo*," Tati managed to say, now dizzy and light-headed with rage.

The buzz of the patrons became distant, and perturbing flashes of Julio returned once again, but this time she was reminded of the wet, warm feel of his lips inviting her full breast to ecstasy. No, no, she said to herself. She felt dizzy and faint. The shoe store seems to suddenly spin around her. Oh God, she was going to faint. She could hear Zuleika's voice in the distance, so far away she thought. She tried to call out for her, but there was no voice in her throat.

"Mami, Mami" Zuleika said, seeing her mother pale and clammy. Tati reached for Zuleika as the red shoe fell slowly onto the brown carpeted floor. Tati followed close behind as she fainted.

As she fell to the floor she sensed the sudden scent of a man, strong, and soothing holding her like a net. She was safe now, she thought. It took only seconds for her to return to her senses as she stared at the brown man with the blue eyes.

"Ay, Mami, are you all right?" Zuleika asked. "You're lucky he caught you. You could've cracked your head." Tati sensed Zuleika's dread and fear.

"I'm ok," Tati said. "*Gracias, Gracias*," she added as she turned her attention to the man with the blue eyes.

"Water," he demanded, and Tati heard people scurrying about in the background. The brown man sat Tati on the beige vinyl chair and he sat next to her. He held her arm. He could see she was still dizzy.

The storeowner, a wiry, silver-haired woman approached him with bay rum, water and camphor stick.

"It's the heat," the blue-eyed man said as he took out his handkerchief from his pocket. He poured bay rum on it and rubbed it on her forehead. He made her smell a piece of white camphor stick the woman handed him.

Tati inhaled the cool scent and composed herself. She

25

apologized for the inconvenience and took several deep breaths.

Zuleika held her hands, relieved that her mother was well.

"I'm fine, Zuki, don't worry," Tati said.

"May I escort you home?" the man asked. "My name is Paino Mejia, *a su servicio.*"

"Yo vivo en el Bronx," Tati managed to say.

"No hay problema," he answered.

"Ok, *sí, sí,* that'll be fine," Tati said, staring at his eyes, the most beautiful eyes she had ever seen.

Zuleika sighed as she noticed the gentle way in which this man cradled her mother's forearm. Secretly, she longed to have fallen in his strong arms, to be engulfed by the woody scent of his fragrance. She continued staring at him, but when he glanced at her and smiled, she saw herself in his eyes, dancing in red shoes.

The Pinocchio
1967

Once upon a time in the Bronx, Rosa, who was six, and Mimi, who was five, lived with their grandmother, *la Guela*, after losing their parents in an auto accident while traveling from Puerto Plata to Santo Domingo. *La Guela* lived in a three-bedroom apartment that had previously been rented by her daughter and son-in-law. She supported herself by sewing and rented one of her rooms to *el Doctor*, Luis Felipe, who had recently arrived from the Dominican Republic. He came to *la Guela* through a respected source, a friend of a relative, and worked in a nearby local hospital. His family remained in Santiago but was soon to join him in the Bronx. *La Guela* felt safer with a man in the house, given the deteriorating conditions of the neighborhood.

One day after school, Luis Felipe came quietly into the girls' bedroom. They lived in an L shaped apartment and so the bedroom was far away from the kitchen where *la Guela* was cooking *garbanzos criollos*, a chick-pea stew with white rice, together with *tostones* and salad.

"*Hola*," he said, but the girls ignored him, their little tummies now yearning for the chick-peas stew they could smell in the distance.

"*Hola*," he repeated.

"Hello," they responded as they jumped on their bed, their arms locked for support and balance. Their thin summer dresses billowed up every time they jumped, revealed their white cotton panties, a little oversized and sagging at the bottom. They noticed how he focused on them, how his eyes glowed at the sight of their little skinny legs, so they jumped higher, until they noticed that he carried a pretty gift bag, probably a present for them. So they stopped jumping.

"What's that?" Rosa asked.

"Gifts," he said, "one for my dark Virgin," looking at Rosa, her mass of full, spiraling, curly hair sloppily cascading

27

across her face. "And one for my light-skinned Virgin," he looked at Mimi with her light skin, hazel eyes and light brown silky hair.

"Can we see it?" Mimi asked.

"Well, well, well," he said hiding the presents behind his back. "First, we must play a special game, and then you may get your wonderful gift."

The girls looked at him, eager to comply.

"But, can we at least see it?" Rosa asked. She was older and bolder and often wanted to make sure that whatever she did would be worth the effort.

"Ok," he said and took out a small dark Virgin figurine he'd bought in the local Botánica for Rosa and then revealed a light-skinned Virgin one for Mimi. Mimi giggled at the sight of her pretty virgin with her blue dress and folded hands. Rosa smiled quietly as she looked at her dark-skinned Virgin who looked so much like her. The scent of the frankincense from the local Botánica permeated the air as he placed the virgins back in their bags.

"They smell sweet," Rosa said smiling.

"They sure do," he answered. "Do you know that if you pray to the virgins, they will give you whatever you want?"

"Really," the girls said and giggled at the thought of wishes coming true.

"But first, the Virgins want you to play a game with me," he said, placing the Virgins on the floor as he sat down on the bed. The girls looked at each other, a wordless cue that signaled their mutual readiness and then they looked at Luis Felipe.

"The Virgins love the silence of little girls," he said as the bed squeaked like a rat. "So we must keep this a secret," he said, his tone growing hushed. "The Virgins will be mad at you if you tell, and something bad might happen you know."

The girls stared at him wide-eyed. "No, no, we won't tell," the girls, responded, thinking of holding their Virgins,

28

playing with them, and praying to them. He touched his index finger to his lips saying, "Shh, you'll tell no one."

"No one," they responded in the same hushed tone. "It's a secret," they added.

Luis Felipe sat on the edge of the bed and explained that the name of the game was Pinocchio.

"Pinocchio?" the girls asked, "Like the story?"

"Yes, but this is a different Pinocchio. This Pinocchio's nose grows and you'll be able to see it and touch it," he said, giggling enthusiastically and gently tickling them on their tummies. The girls giggled. He continued. "Now, every man has a nose like Pinocchio, but in a different place. If you touch it, Pinocchio grows," he said

"Really? Can we see it?" they asked.

"Yes, sure. My Pinocchio is right here," he said, gently guiding their thin hands to the zipper of his pants. The girls felt a hard thing there. They glanced again at each other and giggled.

"Is it growing now?" Rosa asked, wanting to make sure Luis Felipe kept his promise about his Pinocchio growing. Luis Felipe unzipped his pants and proudly displayed his throbbing hard penis.

"Look it's already growing," he said. The girls looked at it like one would look at a strange lizard, trying to understand its shape and form.

"You could touch it, Rosa, and it will grow a little more," he said, and Rosa giggled as she touched it. Mimi immediately grew envious of Rosa. It was always like that, Rosa demonstrating more daring.

"Can I touch it, can I touch it?" Mimi asked, pushing Rosa's hand away from the stiffened Pinocchio, and replacing it with her own.

"Yes, Mimi, stroke it like you do your cat Winky," he said, and she did.

"Yes, yes, like that," he said, his penis now reddening.

Mimi's eyes grew large and she teased Rosa, "Look it grows more when I touch it!"

"No it doesn't," Rosa said disdainfully.

"Yes it did!" Mimi responded.

"Stop, stop, here you can both touch," he said as he took their hands and placed them sequentially around Pinocchio. "Yes, it feels good. You are making Pinocchio very happy," he said. "Oh, yes," he said, "Yes...but...there are other ways to make Pinocchio grow," he said breathlessly. The girls looked at him curiously.

"Well, he likes to be kissed," he said, gently applying a little kiss to Rosa's mouth and then Mimi's.

"You can kiss it like I kissed you," he said, but by then the girls were growing bored. As the scent of the chickpea stew had become more powerful, Rosa told Mimi that dinner must be ready. So they stopped touching Pinocchio. Luis Felipe was disappointed, and at that moment, they heard *la Guela* scream out "Dinner is ready!" Her footsteps could be heard nearing the room. The girls watched how Pinocchio grew small like a worm, and Luis Felipe nervously stuck it inside of his pants and zipped himself just before *la Guela* walked in. The girls went back on their bed and started to jump on the bed as before.

"*Bájense de ahí carambale,*" *la Guela* yelled as she entered the room and ordered the girls off the bed as she wiped her wet hands on her apron.

"*Ay perdone*, Doctor," *la Guela* said and scolded the girls for their disrespect.

The girls came down from the bed. The girls and Luis Felipe slowly followed *la Guela* to the dinner table. There, Luis Felipe prayed "Our father who art in heaven," and he thanked the Lord for all of his blessings as the girls watched him, and *la Guela* said Amen.

Then that night in the warmth of their pajamas, as *la Guela* tucked them and their virgins into bed, they told her about their special game with Luis Felipe, for what was the point of a secret if you couldn't share it with someone special like *la Guela*, but soon their smiles turned to concern when they noticed *la Guela*'s questioning eyes and her pursed unsatisfied lips.

"Pinocchio?" *la Guela* asked as if the name was familiar, but forgotten.

"You must have played it too, Guela," the girls said as they uncovered themselves holding onto their Virgins.

"Eso es un cuento," *la Guela* pointed out as if unsure, and then she remained silent as if remembering. "A story about children who lie."

"No, Pinocchio is down there, Guela," Rosa said and pointed in between her grandmother's thighs.

"And a man's Pinocchio grows and grows," Mimi said extending her arms way beyond all possibilities of growth.

"Miren, carajo," *la Guela* said angrily, *"Eso no se dice! mentirosas,"* and she scolded them for telling lies about Luis Felipe, a respectable young doctor who had a wife and children waiting for him in Santo Domingo.

"Demen las virgenes, Carajole," *la Guela* demanded the Virgins as she noticed the girls holding on to them tightly. So she moved to take them away from the girls, but the girls held onto them tightly.

"No, Guela," they cried, but the Guela continued, *"Demenla,"* she said as she took their Virgins away because children who lied shouldn't have them, *la Guela* said as the girls cried. "You do not deserve the Virgins. Now go to sleep." The girls cried.

"Acuéstense," *la Guela* screamed. *"Acuéstense,"* she demanded and "May God forgive you," she added and left their room in a rush.

That night they cried until they grew tired and their eyes sleepy, but before they fell asleep, they promised that from that moment on everything they did with Luis Felipe would remain a secret.

To Tell the Truth

Mia followed Eva's hurried footsteps angling south towards Fordham Road. The once bruised sky had changed colors and large gray clouds hovered above them like fists waiting to explode upon their heads.

"I can't do this anymore," Mia said.

Eva rolled her eyes at her and puffed, "Forget it then, don't do it. I'll just go with America."

"America?"

"*Sí*, America."

"She's not family, Eva,"

"So, at least she has guts."

America was a Dominican girl with a violin-shaped body too overdeveloped for her thirteen years of age. She spoke English with a heavy accent and her father, Luis Felipe, was the family's local doctor, the one everyone called *el Doctor*. He had a small practice in the Bronx. He kept a tight watch on America, but despite that, she was all over the place kissing boys and touching girls. America was the one older men at the *colmado* turned to look at and meowed like cats when she passed by, as they asked to be scratched by her, *"Aráñáme, Rubia linda,"* they would say. She was the one who knew the power of her charms, who had a preference for girls, and a tolerance for boys.

America loved to love and be loved. She hated school, parental rules, and her name America. Her name was her mother's hope for the promised land, but America didn't think anyone should have a name of a country, state, continent, planet, day of the week, or local object, and if she had to, she would prefer a name that was more to her character. She preferred to be called Rica because in Spanish it meant "rich" and "delicious" and she thought she was all that and more.

"Esa Rica?" Mia said, "Tía Martirio says that by the time she's seventeen she'll have a baby," she added.

"What's a freaking baby, anyway, Mia? If I ever get pregnant I just let Mami take care of the baby. She'll have to."

"*Ay, por Dios*, Eva."

"What is she going to do, give it away? You know how they are. After the shit happens, they're there cleaning it up—that's what family is for, right? Didn't you say that?"

"Eva, it's not like that, you know, not like that, por *Dios*."

Mia hated it when Eva spoke badly about the family.

"You know what your problem is, Mia?"

Mia did not like the tone of her voice.

"What's my problem?" Mia asked in the same tone, and Eva rolled her eyes at her.

"You're problem is that you are just a chickenshit," Eva said and laughed.

"I'm not."

"Yes, you are. You're always afraid of things. You can't live life like that, you know. You have to take a risk."

"I just don't want to do it," Mia said, finding a strength she did not know she had.

"Well, don't go, Mia. I'm not forcing you, you know."

"What if we get caught, Eva?" Mia asked, feeling cold and shivering.

Eva waited for a minute at the traffic light, and when they crossed, she slowed her pace.

"Well, if they ever caught me playing hooky," she laughed at her own words. Then she continued, "I would say that I went to a church for forgiveness from God...*el Dios que* sees everything, right?"

"*Por Dios*, Eva," she said, afraid of God's wrath. What if God punished her because of Eva? No, her father said that God was not a punishing God.

Mia was startled by Eva's cackling laughter, it seemed unreal. Eva jumped up and down as she thought of some other brilliant idea as to how to fool her parents. "I know...I know..." she said as if she were raising her hands in a classroom, "I...I would say..." she giggled and laughed and couldn't say what she wanted to say because she found it hysterically funny and Mia stared at her, waiting. Eva covered her mouth and burst out laughing again, making Mia laugh.

"Come on stupid..." Mia said, hitting her across the arm.

"Ok...Ok...I....would say...I went to church to heal from the evil spirits that cause women to do bad things. Isn't that smart?" she asked, chuckling. "I would say the Devil made me do it. You know how it is," Eva said as they continued to walk the streets of the Bronx towards the train station.

"*Ay, por Dios*, Eva."

"It's that we are so easily influenced by the Devil that the Devil causes us women to do bad things," she added as she laughed, "My holy Father loves shit like that."

"No, you wouldn't."

"Yes, I would. I mean we are completely fucked, Mia," Eva said as she faced her and held Mia by the shoulders.

"There is the Devil that causes us to do bad things and then there's God who punishes us for whatever the hell the Devil made us do. Explain that shit to me.

Mia remained silent.

"Where is forgiveness, Mia, where?" she asked. "I thought God was forgiving, that God saw everything and understood."

"Papi says he does."

"Not in my house. In my house there is the Devil," Eva said, her left hand extended and opened, her palm up at the sky. "And then there is God," she added, putting out her right hand in the same position as the left.

Mia stared at Eva's hands and then at Eva.

"Do you know that it seems like the Devil and God are doing the same old job. It's just that one feels that because he is God, he can punish me because I am a woman, and I am easily influenced by the Devil. Don't you find something wrong with that shit?"

"*Por Dios*, Eva…" Mia said. For sure God was going to punish them, she thought, and so she implored God's forgiveness by looking up at the sky and saying, "God don't listen to her, please," and then she prayed silently for God's forgiveness.

They walked quietly down the steps of the dark train station and into the coolness of the tunnel like the mouth of a whale. They showed their train passes to the fat dark man in the booth and passed through the wooden doors onto the platform. The scent of urine and marijuana permeated the air as they walked down yet another set of steps towards the downtown train. There was no one on the platform and in the distance Mia could hear the roar of a train that had just left. She was disappointed. She wanted to go to her beautiful room, all in white and pink, and find comfort in her parents' belief that she was still a child and knew nothing about love or about boys.

Eva began to look for something in her coat pocket and then in her school bag. She knelt on the floor with her bag and started searching. Mia knew she was looking for her cigarettes.

"*Ay, por Dios*, Eva, if a cop saw you we'd get a ticket you know."

Eva took a deep drag from the cigarette and held the smoke in her lungs. "*La mujer que sabe fumar bota el humo despues de hablar,*" she repeated, holding the smoke deep in her chest, an exercise that would teach them to inhale the smoke and hold it deep in the lungs while they said "The woman who knows how to smoke exhales the fumes after she speaks." Eva blew smoke in her face, and Mia fanned it away. She looked at Eva with disgust. She thought of when she first tried to smoke, how she'd often choke. Her lungs were weak and unable to hold the smoke deep inside, and what was the purpose—she didn't find anything fun in it.

Often, she'd get dizzy, nauseous, and want to throw up. Then she would have to lie down until the dizzy spell passed.

"Give me the cigarette," she said, but Eva ran away from her and their voices echoed in the dark tunnel.

"Shh, Eva, shh," she said, but Eva just took a deep drag again and blew the smoke in her face and she coughed.

"You're like two different people, Eva. If your parents only knew," she said as she moved away from her, but she smiled because she admired Eva's strength, her determination and her wickedness. "You're wicked, Eva."

"I'm wicked, wicked, come on and lick it," Eva sang as she ran to Mia and humped her on her hip, holding her cigarette away from Mia's potential grab.

"Your father will exorcise that wickedness out of you," she said.

"God," Eva screamed out into the air "I want to lick life."

"Evelina, *por Dios*, shh, shh." She tried to repress Eva's desires and longings and her own envy of them. Eva hugged her and tried to lick her cheeks.

"Stop it, *puerca*," Mia said pushing her away and laughing. She stared at Eva who was still talking about licking things and licking life.

"This is too much for me," Eva said and stopped laughing and added "It's freaking 1972 and we're not allowed friends, or boyfriends. We must rebel. We must take life into our own hands," and she made Mia laugh.

The train arrived and they entered the old art deco car with its wooden frame, and they sat in the cushiony old burgundy leather seats. She felt comforted by its familiar feel. Mia spoke about Rica and her disappointment that she stayed behind with the boys. Wasn't Eva worried? Eva shrugged it off.

They were silent for a moment thinking about things that their families would not approve of. Mia felt cuddled by the motion of the train and noticed how sleepy she was. She thought of the blood that flowed down her legs, the beginning of everything different now that she was a *señorita*.

"Isn't life weird, Eva?"

"In what way?"

"There are so many restrictions to being a *señorita*, right?"

"Yup."

"You can't do this."

"Yup! And you can't do that," Eva said.

"Everything is a problem. My mom said that when a woman's blood flows, she has to be *en reposo*, that you can't run around or play."

"Yup, and you can't eat this or that."

"Well, she said we can't drink lemonade because it'll stop the flow," Mia said.

"And what is it with the feet?"

"Oh, yeah, you must put on your *chancletas* because the floor is too cold," Eva said and made Mia laugh.

"And don't wash your hair."

"And put on a hat."

"And you can't be with boys."

"Yeah, yeah," Mia said.

"What, are we going to contaminate them?" she asked.

"Really."

She recalled how one day she was particularly happy and went to sit on her father's s lap and he pushed her away. "I'm sorry," he said as he explained that now that she was a *señorita*, she could no longer sit on his lap. She glanced at his lap, the lap that had brought so much comfort throughout the years, the lap that had rocked her to sleep and had comforted her after a fall.

Eva took out a lollipop and began to suck it as she spoke. Mia stared at Eva as the lollipop turned from a dry red color to a luscious wet one, and Eva twirled it in and out of her mouth with great expertise. She though of Eva, how everything she did had so much passion in it, even the licking of a simple lollipop. Then, Eva startled Mia by bursting out laughing even before she spoke, and in a burst of giggles, Eva said, "Do you know that when boys feel good, milk comes out of their…?" Eva laughed as she said this, and her saliva spilled from her mouth onto her chin and some of it on Mia's face.

"*Puerca*," Mia said to her and punched her on the shoulder. Eva wiped herself with the back of her right hand and put her lollipop back into her mouth as she spoke in a muffle, her tongue twirling on it as she spoke about boys, the unique function of a penis and the power of the milk that spilled from it. Mia was mesmerized. She knew nothing of a girl's or boy's body, about vaginas and penises. These things were not discussed. What she knew, she learned from Eva who was older, and who despite having to repeat the seventh grade, she was smart when it came to boys.

"Yeah, and the milk…" Eva continued, her lips sweet and sticky from the juice of the lollipop.

Eva continued enlightening Mia about boys and their sexuality while Mia thought about the family, how they never told them anything about sex, although they could have babies now. Adults were stupid, she thought, and when she had her own daughter, she'd tell her everything so that she would not be blind about her body, regretting her actions later when it was too late. Mia found all her misinformation in school through her friends, stupid nonsense about the diversity of a woman's private parts, how some *pompos* were better than others because the slit was crooked, horizontal or vertical, and that not all women's vaginas were the same—that some had long soft hair, while others were Brillo prickly, and that American vaginas were all blonde. One of her friends said that men like white women because they had a knowing eye right in the middle of their vaginas.

Eva's words brought Mia back to the present. This thing about men spilling milk like a cow out of their private parts was as bizarre as a white woman having a knowing eye in the middle of their vaginas.

"I can't believe it, Eva, that's so weird. A bin-bin that spills milk."

Eva looked at her in disbelief, "*Por Dios* Mia, you still call a dick a bin-bin? Please! Come here, say Diiiicckckkk" Eva said, holding Mia's cheeks. "Dick!"

"Get away, it's not dick, anyway."

"Dick."

"*Pene*, it's *pene*."

"No, dick."

"Stop it, Eva," Mia said and smacked her hand away from her cheeks.

"Ok, *Pene*, then, but stop calling a woman's vagina "pompo." It's a vagina."

"I'll call it that …when I'm ready, Eva," Mia whispered.

They giggled for a moment and then Mia whispered, "Wow, Eva, so they spill milk like a cow?"

"I never thought of it like that, but yeah like a cow."

"How does the milk come out and all?"

"Well, first a boy has to be with a woman. It has to be fun, like playing around and shit," Eva said.

"But tell me, tell me more."

"Well, it all relates to your menstrual cycle. If you bleed every month, it's ok, but if you don't, it means you're pregnant."

"What does that have to do with him?"

"Well, you know that the ovary puts out an egg."

"Like a chicken?"

"Like a chicken."

"That egg and the white stuff from a man will make a baby."

"Yeah, I think I heard that."

"Yeah, that's why it's dangerous, and if that milk gets near you, *mi'jita*, you'll have a baby."

"Can you get pregnant from a kiss?"

"No, dummy."

"How about from a touch?"

"No, silly, I told you that white thing has life in it, everything you need to have a baby, but it has to find your egg inside of you."

"Yuk, so that white thing has to go deep inside me?"

"Yes."

"Wow, so they have milk that comes out when they feel good and we bleed and have painful cramps. What a life," Mia said.

Eva laughed, and Mia drifted into her own thoughts. Suddenly, she felt confused about the truth, about the world and its expectations, for she was not a woman, nor a child, and the elders around her were also confused and confusing. There was no one to help. All of this and no one to help her understand that the world had confusing expectations for girls, and left the world free for boys to grow.

When they arrived, Eva and Mia walked briskly, ignoring old friends waving, and just hoping to get home safe and sound. So many times they had played hooky and arrived home and no one knew. Playing hooky wasn't something that stayed stamped on your forehead. Mia would kiss her mother hello if she were home, and they would continue their normal routine. Her mother would arrive early from her part-time job, and she'd be sad and silent in the kitchen peeling *plátanos* while her brother hung out with his friends in the park. Everything would be normal; everything would be just as before.

Once they reached the double-sided building, they stopped and stared at it; it looked so quiet and silent. They entered holding hands tightly. They could hear the sounds of hurried footsteps in the hallway, like soldiers marching, but they knew it was the footsteps of relatives.

They reached the second floor and were confronted by Eva's mother, Virtudes, her eyes swollen and small; she stared at them, but didn't say anything. Eva's older brothers, Wagner, and Tía Socorro were guarding Mia's mother, Dolores, as if she were about to collapse. Tía Martirio stared at them and threatened to smack them. "*Carajo*," she'd said and went on and on about the state of the world.

Mia realized they were in trouble, big trouble. She knew then that her teacher had called as she had threatened to do. She took in a deep breath, but couldn't exhale. For a moment she thought she would faint.

Everything seemed large to Mia, people's faces and their hands. Their voices were like muffled echoes from a distance, and she could not decipher the meaning of their mumbled words. She felt unreal, as if she no longer existed, as if she were already dead.

She stared at Tía Virtudes, whose eyes were red from crying. She had disappointed her. Tío Quinto stood stoically in the maroon art deco hallway. He held his 5 x 7 leather bound zipper bible, the old tattered one, with worn onionskin pages with red edges like blood. Their whispering voices sounded like a swarm of bees and Mia wanted to run and hide.

Mia's mother and father began to argue. She could hear in the distance her mother's muffling cries. Tati interrupted their argument and argued with Suarez.

"*No le hagas caso*," Tati said about Tío Quinto who insisted that the Devil had some part in their behavior.

"*No hay ningún demonio.*"

Mia could hear the word Devil and her mother's sobs.

Her mother knew that Tío Quinto was an extremist, and they did not have to go by his rules. In the distance her father responded "*una lección*"—he had to teach her a lesson. In Tío Quinto's rules of conduct, a woman's worth was validated by her virginity, and it was clear that if Mia was out there playing hooky she might have lost hers. This was unacceptable; they had not come to the land that promised prosperity to have their children end up pregnant, children having children. Mia's father walked out of the apartment into the hallway.

"*Espera adentro.*" He said, and he walked towards Eva knowing that for the fear of God she would never lie.

"*Esa Eva te dice la verdad.*" Mia could hear her uncle saying in the distance. Eva always says the truth, she is "good," he said, "*muy buena*" and too frightened of adults, of God's wrath, to ever lie.

"*Ven aca.*" Her father said to Eva and asked her to come out and speak to him. He said this respectfully and looked at Eva with love and compassion as if he did not want to frighten her. Mia watched them as they spoke. Her father paced the hallway where he spoke with Charlie, Tío Quinto and the whole family stood frozen, her mother next to Tati, and Tía Martirio with Rosa and Mimi. Aura came from la Botánica, and ran towards Mia, but Tío Quinto stopped her.

Mia looked around, her mind racing. She saw her grandmother, *la Guela*, with the younger children, little boys that did not know what was really going on. Why did they all have to be here? she wondered.

Zuleika, who was a freshmen in Taft High School, came rushing in, her light brown hair a mass of soft curls across her pretty face. The family spoke about American culture, about how the country was falling apart and how it was time to leave. There was no promise here, they said.

Everyone whispered and the children's heartbeats could be heard as if the trouble involved them, as if they too would get punished, and Mia could smell the sweat of the women in her family. It smelled like crushed garlic. Their voices boomed and echoed in the hallways, and the old white ladies opened their doors slightly, wondering if there was a fire or a burglary.

"If we don't do something now, Suarez, these girls will just go on disrespecting us, ending up like prostitutes or drug addicts with the Devil."

"Por Dios." Aura said, "Can we leave the Devil out of this."

"They are possessed," Tío Quinto said.

"They are young girls who need guidance," Aura said.

"They are women first," Tío Quinto reminded him, "And women are weak. Weak and easily influenced by the Devil to seduce and create havoc in this world. A lesson is needed, and one they won't forget."

She could see how her father wiped the sweat off his forehead with his right hand. Mia stood there in the entrance of her apartment. She wanted to run past them, run far away to a place where she would be safe. The family wasn't safe, but where would she go? Her legs couldn't move. She was like a mouse trapped by a cat.

This is a dream, she thought, God, wake me up, she said to herself. She could see that her uncle and father were now talking to Eva again, and Eva answered back, but she did so in a whisper, so Mia couldn't hear at all. Eva seemed scared for the first time in her life, and she lowered her eyes out of respect as she spoke to them. Mia tried to hear Eva's answers, but she couldn't. God she wished she could hear. All she saw were Eva's familiar hand gestures and her lowered eyes and moving lips.

Everyone stood in the hallway, the children asking what was wrong.

"Who died?" someone asked.

Mia stood immobile in the hallway of the apartment. Her legs barely able to hold her shaking body, her heart hammering. After a few minutes that seemed an eternity, the family walked in and gathered semi-circle in the living room area.

Her father grabbed Mia by the blouse and threw her into the middle of the living room. She wondered what Eva had said because her father was furious. He had never grabbed her like that. The door outside slammed shut, and then her mother Dolores stood next to her husband. The apartment was still, silent and warm. Mia could smell the pine-sole scent of the floor, which was overwhelmed by the aroma of the *arroz con pollo.*

There was a somber silence, and only the tick of the clock could be heard.

"Where were you today?"

"I was in school," she lied.

"Mia I asked you, where were you?" he said, emphasizing the *where were you.*

"I was in school."

"You are lying," he screamed.

He asked the same question again and again. She didn't tell. She lied like Eva said to.

"Where were you, Mia?"

Mia cried and muttered, "In the park, I was in the park."

Suddenly, her father slapped her. She heard her mother cry "*Ay, Dios mío, por favor.*" But she could not move to save her life. She felt the trickle of blood coming from her nose. She started to scream and wiped her nose with her hands.

"You were with boys, right?"

Mia looked at Eva, whose eyes were telling her to continue lying.

"No, no boys, Papi."

"You are lying."

"I'm not." She said, whimpering. "I swear."

"You were with boys."

"No, Papi, no," she said, crying and begging him for mercy. "I'll talk to you alone, Papi, but not in front of everyone."

"You were with boys, right?"

"No, no, I wasn't with boys."

He took the belt from his pants and belted the floor four times, then five, and then one strong whip to her leg. Mia felt the whip like salt on an open wound, and she jumped at the blow, but on the next whip, the tip of the belt struck Mia in the eye, making her jump and scream, "Papi, no, no," as she covered her bleeding eye.

Some of the kids laughed as they watched her; others were scared.

"You are stubborn. Tell me the truth," he said.

"I'm telling you the truth," she said.

"Are you?"

"I told you."

"*Coño, carajo,* what have I taught you, Ynoemia, I've given you everything, everything I have, everything you need," he said in Spanish. "*Para que tú me hagas esto, carajo.* Now, you are nothing, now you are as good as nothing, all broken up and a liar. How dare you do this to me, how dare you do this to your family?"

Mia covered her face in shame. She regretted her actions. She knew she should never have played hooky with Eva. She was so ashamed, and she knew her family was witness to her shame, and that life after this would never be the same. Her family watched quietly, silently.

Tío Quinto prayed and the children laughed out of fear. The women watched, afraid to defy her father. It was his daughter, and she was his property.

"I'll ask you one last time," he said. "Where were you, Ynoemia?"

"I was with boys," she confessed.

"Where?"

"The park."

"You're lying."

"The park."

"Tell me the truth. I want to hear it from you," he said as if he had heard the truth from someone else.

Mia looked at Eva through her blurred vision and to her surprise Eva was crying. She looked like a virgin in disguise. Her face angelic, her body and behavior like a child's. Suddenly she knew about betrayal. It was such a brutal betrayal, she thought. She was alone in the world.

She didn't want to answer, but in a whisper said, "In their apartment."

"So it's true what Eva said?"

"What?"

"That you lock yourself with the boys in their room, Ynoemia, what have we taught you. What?"

"No. No."

"That you were doing things, fresh things with those boys."

"No, no...Eva...Please tell the truth." She glanced towards Eva and stood from the floor to beg Eva, but Tío Quinto didn't let her get close to her.

"So it's true that Eva just sits there watching television while you lock yourself in the bedroom with the boys?"

"Never, never, ask Rica, Papi, she'll tell you the truth."

"Now, you're getting Rica involved in this too."

"No, Pá, ask her. Please, Papi, have faith in me, and don't believe something like that." Her face was hurting and swollen and she was spitting blood. In the distance she could hear her cousin Zuki crying. Her mother stood still. She heard Tati urge her mother to stop the punishment, but her mother just stood still and did nothing.

"You've lied about everything else," her father said, "so why should we believe you?"

"*Papi, por Dios*, no, I'm just thirteen years old, just thirteen," she said, tears streaming down her cheeks. For a moment, she thought, that her voice brought her father back to her. She could hear his regret in the crack of his voice.

"Maybe I've gone too far," he said, "Maybe I will some day regret it, but the damage is done. We did not come to the United States to raise whores."

"*No es justo.*" Tati said and Aura chimed in, trying once again to reach Mia. "This was not the right way to teach a lesson, it wasn't right. Would they do the same with the boys if they made a mistake, would they?"

"*No te meta en esto, Aura,*" her father said, keeping both

Aura and Tati at bay before they could reach Mia, who was crying on the floor.

"Let her lie there in shame. I want her to know that I no longer believe in her, I want her to know that I don't love her anymore."

Mia listened to those words and knew that no matter what happened, they were words that would remain in her heart forever—words that would echo around her mind and soul for a long time to come. He did not love her anymore.

There was a silence for a while.

"You don't know what you are saying, Suarez," Tati spat at him, and he glanced toward her as if he would smack her, too.

Aura ran to Mia.

"Let her go Aura; don't touch her, Tati. I don't want anyone speaking to her for six days. Whoever speaks to her runs the risk of the same punishment."

Mia glanced towards him as he gave out his sentence. This was the father who once loved her. How strange it was that this man could be the same man who adored her. She lay there on the floor, crying in her shame.

The Awakening

El Paso de Mano

Aura arrives with her frankincense and her mysteries. Her scent of wet earth, and crushed flowers, a touch of jasmine and hibiscus. Her dark hands passing over my body, her warmth. A whisper. A prayer.
I stir.
The energy of her hands passes through me.
Un paso de mano.
In the distance, my grandmother, *la Guela*, hums while she boils herbs with Berron, and Vivaporu. The Vicks Vapor Rub and the Bay Rum making a warm substance they rub on my body, their hands full of love, healing my brokenness.
Now the cool scent of their magic brew awakens me. I stir, open my eyes. I move , but I can't get up. Aura sprinkles *Agua de Florida* to bring healing spirits my way. They pray.
"Ave Maria, Madre de Dios... ruega por nosotras."
Ruega por nosotras. Their love awakens me.

Forgetting is Easy

Forgetting is easy. I close my eyes, and I don't think of the beating, yet I find that my body remembers as if memories can lock themselves inside of me, remind me of the past. I feel fear and pain. I close my eyes to forget and I dream. Sometimes, I dream of Pito. Pito's hands gliding up my thigh, his warm lips upon mine. I dream of Eva.
I try to forget them.
Lately I move and walk and eat again, but I do not feel the same. There is something different inside of me. There is something broken. Sometimes, the elders will ask, "What's wrong, Mia?" Grown ups, they ask stupid questions all the time. They cut your arm and then they ask, "Does it hurt?"

"*Habla un chin, un chin chin,*" Zuleika says. She wants me to speak a little bit, but I write to her that I can't. That's how it all begins. I write in this notebook.

I write and writing comforts me.

Invisible Bruises

My room is black. A blue black like a bruise. Black walls and black carpet with psychedelic colors, dark blue bedspread and a lamp that makes rainbows on the black walls. The ceiling is red like blood and when I lie down on my bed, that blood-red reminds me of the past. Mami cried when she saw the room black. Mami who loves everything white, whose bathroom is so white and clean you can eat on the floor. She says black is a beautiful color, but not for a bedroom. I have dark shades that don't let the sun in. Sometimes, I wake up and I have no light in my heart, no hope. I feel a deep sadness as if someone died. It is an awful feeling that doesn't go away. I open my eyes, and I wonder about living.

Death. It's too final.

Aura comes to tell me stories. Stories about our ancestor, los Taíno Indians, or Yoruba stories about Yemaya, Oshun, Elegua and Obatala. She shares the mysteries with me, the knowledge of the spiritual world. Sometimes I listen, but other times, even stories make me sad. I look away. I sit on the windowsill of the fire escape, and I see my reflection staring at me.

It's an ugly reflection.

Today, I am covered with bruises. I see bruises all over my body, although it's been a long time since the beating. Some of the bruises are fading now, but others stay to remind me. They are now all sorts of colors—blue, purple, pink, and yellow. A sick-looking yellow. My face is the same, but if you look closer you will see that my left side of my face is swollen with sorrow. I write this down for Zuki in my notebook.

Zuki reads this and says, "You don't have any bruises, Mia, Tío only hit you once,"

I realize now how different memory is from one person to another. I feel he hit me a lot, but she says he didn't, so I don't know what the truth is.

Aura walks in with Mimi and Rosa.

Zuki asked them "Do you see bruises on her?"

They come close.

Rosa and Mimi stare at my bruises, but they can't see them.

Aura looks at me and says, "I think she has bruises, it's just that we don't see them."

I sigh deeply and feel relieved.

Aura believes that people could have bruises on their body; it's just that normal eyes can't see them because the bruises are invisible. She says that loss can cause bruises, losing the mother you love, or the father you love, losing something important.

We stay quiet when she speaks.

She says that words can cause invisible bruises, too. "Bruises, can be deep, deep inside of your heart." She points to my heart. "And there the bruises hide, causing a tangle of sadness. If left alone and misunderstood, this sadness can be like your shadow you take everywhere. "

We nod.

"It can change the way you see life, love, people," she says.

"How can you see them?" Zuki asks.

"Look very slowly and stay still," she says and places her fingers on her lips.

"For bruises to be visible you have to be silent. Still. Shh...shh... and then they begin to be visible. You have the magic, all of you do to see invisible bruises. Wait. Listen. See..."

I stay still, watching them all, and I begin to see. I see Mimi and Rosa have bruises.

The others remain quiet. Mimi has her eyes closed and Rosa is attentive. Waiting. We are quiet. My family is full of secrets. They rarely speak about their past or their beginnings. The women in my family do not share anything about their history.

My mother comes into the room and she's followed by her sister, Tía Socorro.

"*¿Que están haciendo?*"

I can see their bruises too. I guess we all have bruises, bruises that become invisible when we cannot name them.

Palabras Dulce

When I cross the streets to go to the *colmado* to buy candy, I think the men there know about me. I wonder if they see that I have bruises and that I am burdened with the weight of my sadness, so I don't go out.

My father. He comes. He tries. He wants me to trust him.

When my cousins play dolls, he urges me to play with them. When they are outside playing rope, he wants me to go. He'll say, "Go, go with your cousins downstairs" as if he trusts me, but he doesn't really. He tries to. He wants to. I look out of the window, and I can see the courtyard where my cousins play. They sing an old Dominican song about men.

"No se lleven de los hombres, bres, bres, que son echo de alfileres, res, con sus palabritas dulce, ce, ce, engañando a las mujeres, res, res..."

I find myself feeling joy in watching them and laugh. I am startled by the sound of my voice. I sing, softly to myself in Spanish.

"Do not believe in men, men, men, who are made of needles, needles, needles, with their sweet words, words, words, fooling women, women, women…"

I always wondered who wrote that Dominican childhood song.

The Talking Board

Papi comes by with his sweet voice in the hope of hearing mine, but I do not speak.

I smile.

On the weekends he takes me out everywhere, to the Market or Chinatown for medicines. He buys me everything I want, hoping that I will speak. So I ask for a lot of things— a dream book dictionary to understand the meaning of my dreams, the witchcraft book to understand the power of the mind, *Las Barajas* to read my future, and a book of prayers to change my destiny. Then one day, in hopes of hearing me speak again, he buys me a Talking Board. A beautiful wooden shiny Ouija Board he found in Woolworth.

Now I can speak to the dead, and the dead, they speak back to me.

At night, I touch the planchette of the Ouija board. I ask the dead all sorts of question, usually about Pito. Then I wait, and then it moves under my hands, slowly from one letter of the alphabet to another, a shuffle here and there, and then it quickly jumps to the smiling sun, a "yes," The spirits from the other side are always here. They tell me things about their deaths and speak to me in a language that is hard to understand. Just yesterday, a young woman who died when she was twenty two told me, *mis manos narran la leyenda azul,* that her hands narrate a blue legend. The next morning, the Ouija board was aching for me to talk to it, and when I did, it wrote, *hay historias en mis lágrimás*, that there are stories in tears. I thought, there truly are stories in one's tears. Aura says, "Don't be afraid, spirits are here to help you. Trust their guidance." She says to be patient and write what I hear in my notebook, and I do.

I want to be like Aura who works at the Botánica selling sweet herbs, who understands the language of the spirit world. She can cure illness and create potions that can heal brokenness. I want to stir up the dead from their resting place and talk to them about life and love. I want to know the mysteries of the world.

So, I listen.

La Ciguapa es Guapa

I sleep and dream a lot. Aura says to listen to my dreams, that they have secret gifts sent to me by my ancestors. In my dreams, I hear *La Ciguapa* eating from the refrigerator. I hear her backward footsteps and her long hair sweeping the floor. I close my eyes when her feet come close to my room. She enters and I hold my breath. I fear her only because my family said that she's ugly and short with backward feet and hungry.

La Ciguapa does not speak, but I hear, her voice in my head. She says my name, "Y-no-e-mia…Mia…Mia…," but I do not answer her. Her hands are small, soft, warm to the touch and they are at my feet. She smells of pine, wood, and earth. The fear of my childhood vanishes, and I open my eyes to see her. She has a beautiful childlike face, large eyes and long dark shiny hair. She brings me gifts: a mermaid's comb, a cinnamon stick, and a *guanábana*, but when I go out to take them, I awaken.

I wonder if she, like me, has been misunderstood, if lies have been told about her. *Ciguapa. Ci* - Yes, *Guapa* - Beautiful…. Maybe she is beautiful after all.

I leave her fruit at night next to the gifts she left me that exist only in my dreams.

La Libreta de Los Espíritus

Aura comes, and I write in my notebook about the Ouija board. She calls my notebook, *"la libreta de los espíritus,"* the notebook of spirits.

It is there that I write what I read on the talking board, but it is also the notebook I use to communicate with my family. Papi brought me this notebook on one of our weekend trips to Canal Street. It's a handmade notebook from China with thin brown sheets.

"The spirits say things that are funny," I tell her, and find myself speaking. Aura does not stir, but I see her surprise in her eyes. I give her the notebook.

"Let's see," she says and takes the notebook and opens it. I point out to the pages where I write the spirit's words. *"Bailamos en la risa de la luna,"* she reads out loud and smiles. "Can a person dance to the laughter of the moon?" I wonder, but do not ask her.

"Mi sombrero está cansado dormir," she reads.

"He was killed," I say.

"Yes, I am sure. They are all dead. Right?"

"Yes," I say and begin to realize that they are dead, although their spirits seem so close to me. Aura reads it out loud and laughs. "And this?" she points out hoping to hear me speak again. I look at the notebook. She can't understand my writing, and I read it. *"Mis manos narrar la leyenda azul,"* I say and hear my voice. I start to feel good and safe as Aura listens to me. Aura continues to read, *"Hay historias en mis lágrimas,"*

Aura asks me to read and I do, telling her the story of the spirit that communicates with me, *"El pasado tiene una sonrisa."*

That's from an old man, who passed away, and he thinks a lot about his wife. Do you think the past can have a smile?" I ask.

"If it is a good past."

"See this." I show her *"la espalda del silencio tiene un secreto."* This man was shot in the back. I didn't know that silence could have a back and that a back can have a secret.

"It's like a shadow," Aura says, "The shadow we carry can have a secret."

"Oh, I guess. How about this one? This woman will not tell me how she died; she just wrote, *Los hombres con dedos sin ojos y lágrimas de navajas, tienen miedo.* Aura moves her fingers, and Mia looks for eyes in them, and they laugh.

"Can fingers have eyes?" I ask.

"They might."

"Can tears be like blades?"

"Why not?"

"Can they have fear?"

"I'm sure."

Sometimes the spirits are quiet.

Mis Muertos y Espíritus

I return to childhood. My cousins and I are playing with dolls like little girls. The elders are relieved. We are *niñas* once again, although blood arrives monthly from between our *pompos*, and Rosa's and Mimi's breasts are rivaling Eva's who's storing milk for the baby that is to come.

Tía Martirio doesn't treat me right. When she decided to adopt Rosa and Mimi, who lost their parents, they became her daughters, and I became nothing to her. Rosa and Mimi picked up on this and do the same. Sometimes. One day, they are sweet and other times, mean and cruel.

The girls asked me to bring the Talking Board to play

with the spirits from the other side, but Tía Martirio sent me back.

"Váyase para su casa con sus muertos y espíritus."

She tells me to run home with my dead ones and my spirits. I am stunned and I walk away with my Ouija Board tucked under my arm. I don't tell her what the spirits tell me about Tío Rodrigo, why he comes late from work. I don't tell her what Mimi and Rosa do with Rica's father, *el Doctor*, or what he likes to do with children. I don't tell her anything.

I keep silent, but one day I will tell her.

El Silencio es Peligroso

Today, I am a good girl. I leave the Talking Board home, and the *Las Barajas* in their blue pouch, and I don't even bring my spirit notebook. I leave that, too. Today, I go and play with Rosa and Mimi because *el Doctor* brought them new Barbies and they wanted me to see them. We are playing quietly because Mimi and Rica are making the Barbies do fresh stuff, one on top of the other, and they smile at each other when they do it. I stay quiet because Tía Martirio will blame me. Suddenly, I hear her from the kitchen as she's grounding the seasoning in a *Pilón*, olive oil, oregano, garlic cloves, and salt, humping the *Pilón* in the mortar, I hear her saying, *"Están muy callada,"* and then the sound of the *Pilón*, hump, hump and hump, while Mimi and Rosa are giggling and Tía says, *"El silencio es peligroso,"* silence is dangerous. When we don't respond, Tía comes running into the bedroom, drying her hands with a yellow kitchen towel, the scent of oregano, garlic, oil and vinegar permeating the air. I smile at her, but she looks at me with an evil eye. She says, "I'm watching you," and points at me as if her stepdaughters are good, and she walks away in a huff. I realize that she never says that to the boys. When boys are quiet in one room, they are supposed to be doing something very important, but when we girls are quiet, we are dangerous.

When Tía walks in and out, I notice that Mimi steals my Barbie dresses, and when I want them back, she says they were hers. Rosa comes to protect her and pushes me, "Leave my sister alone," and suddenly I wish I had a sister, about my age, who could protect me, who could defend me when I am in trouble, but I don't. I have a big sister, but she's married and lives in Providence, Rhode Island.

I wonder if I should fight them, but I get afraid because they're crazy when they get mad. Mimi likes to trash things when she gets mad and Rosa likes to punch and kick until she or her enemy is bleeding, and I don't feel like getting hurt. They are cruel, too, calling me names when they are angry, names like *"nalga sucia"* and then the next morning they'll apologize and remind me that family is family, and they want to be my friend again. They'll call me sweet names like *"Manita"* and patch things up until the next time we fight. They are both like Yo Yo's - you never know if you are up or down with them.

But I decide to confront them.

"Give me the dress."

They call me names, and then they have the nerve to get my private parts into the discussion, saying that my pussy stinks, but that's not true because I wash it every morning and night as we are supposed to do.

They called me names whore, *desgraciá,* and say I'm not part of the family. Rosa said that my mother didn't want me because I didn't belong to her. I ignore her. I ignore lies that come out of anger.

"Recogía," they say, but I don't know where they get those ideas. Ideas to make me feel I don't belong to this family, but that's ok. When I don't listen to them, they start chanting my name as if it were a curse, "y-no- e-mia" and "y-no- e-mia" and "y-no- e-mia." They say it slower and

slower until I hear the secret of my self… "she is not mine," but I pay them no mind, although I began to wonder about it.

I chant back to Mimi. "Mimi…Mimi…me…me… me…me..me.." to bother them and Rosa throws her shoe at me and hits me on the eye. I feel it swelling. I walk away with my chest heavy with sadness and I promise myself I will never trust them for the rest of my life.

"Recogía, recogía, recogía," they say, "Not even your father loves you."

For a moment I stand still, and then a deep anger surfaces within me and I run back into their apartment and start to break everything precious to them. We hit each other and pull each other's hair and when I can escape their grasp I run with their Barbies in hand and I flush the Barbies down the toilet. They wouldn't flush, but I gave them a good bath.

I couldn't believe that it was me, that I could be so angry and that I could be so violent. In an instant I broke everything around me. Tía Martirio came and grabbed me by the hair and slammed my head against a wall and brought me back to my senses. I lost my balance and then she threw my dizzy body out into the hallway, her voice echoes as she said, *"Sal de aqui muda e mierda,"* that I was a stupid mute, but I didn't care anymore. I walked away and heard Mimi and Rosa crying, and a sense of triumph swelled from a deep place in my heart.

I didn't know I had this rage, this anger inside of me, and suddenly I felt my voice, my voice came out loud as a scream, a scream that shook the whole building, and Tía Martirio said I was going crazy and she was calling my mother. I didn't feel fear. I suddenly felt alive again and joyful. This time I walked out of the apartment feeling good, and confidant. I had found my voice.

When I walked down to my apartment, I felt an opening inside like I had never felt. Surrounded by my spirits and my newfound joy, I felt as if I had awakened. The breaking, the hitting made me feel so happy. Then I was exhausted, I sat on the steps of the stairs, my face swollen and red, and my hair filled with static electricity and pulled up on one side. Some of it fell off as I smoothed it. I felt a bump surfacing on my head, a big, huge bump, and I touched it to soothe it, but it hurt, and then I heard Tía Virtudes and the pregnant Virgin, Eva, coming up the stairs. Tío wants to believe that Eva is the miracle of conception, that she carries the savior, only because *el Doctor* said that the doors of her Pompo private parts have not been open. If only he knew that there are no miracles anymore.

I could hear her panting, her breathe shallow as she came up the steps with her mother, but, when I saw her I felt that joy again, and I smacked her across the face so hard it blew them both away. I smacked her for betraying me, for lying and saying I was with boys when it was she and Rica who humped on the water bed with Snake, who smoked the sweet herbs that they rolled up in onion paper, who said she would lie her ass off if she was caught playing hooky, and who hated the family for all of their traditions and strictness. I smacked her for that and for so much more, and I felt good. Then I ran.

I ran down the steps with a joy so sweet in my lips and my hands, it traveled through my body and made me want to scream with joy, but my new found happiness soon ended when my mother was waiting for me at the door and smacked me really hard across my face, my joy spilling on the floor and breaking into tiny pieces, my new found voice startled out of me.

"*¿Pero tú te estás volviendo loca?*" she asked, as if I had gone crazy.

"I hate them," I said, startled by the sound of my own voice. I can speak.

"Hating is not allowed in this family, do you hear me," she said "So get rid of that hatred in your eyes,"

I wanted to say it was joy in my eyes, not hatred, but I

wouldn't speak to her. She startled the voice of my happiness out of me, bringing me back to silence. I couldn't move. What does hatred become when it is not allowed in your family? Hatred, an emotion like any other.

Love. Anger.

I walked right past her and went to my room to deal with my hatred, my joy, and my voice. I curled up like a baby on my bed that smells like roses and the sweet scents of la Botánica, and as I fall asleep, I hear my mother speaking on the phone, saying to Tía Martirio, *"Igualita a la Mai'*— that I was just like my mother as if she was not mine.

A Naked Eye Has Lost its Wings

My mom likes boys more than girls, and she gets all crazy when any of her nephews visit. She makes perfect *tostones* and perfect flans for them, and the sweet, blubbery tanned sweet plantain are all for my brother Charlie. Charlie who is so beautiful with his light brown hair that in the summer sun looks blonde, *el rubio*, with his eyes a dusty color of the sky. She makes one whole plantain for him.

When the boys come, she sits and talks to them, and all you hear is her laughter in the distance. I like to hear it, thinking it is with me that she is laughing. I imagine that it is me she loves. She is full of questions, and laughter around them, but sadness surrounds me. When she calls my name, "Ynoemia," it always sounds like she's scolding me even when she is asking a question. I often act as if I haven't heard her. Then my father will say, "Mia, your mother's speaking to you" and then I listen.

I don't speak to my mother so she calls Rica's father, Luis Felipe, *el Doctor de la familia.* Mami treats him like royalty because he's a doctor. But what she doesn't know is that he is a sick doctor. She trusts him because he's educated, but adults don't seem to see through people like him—that underneath his knowledge of the world, underneath his oath to God to heal, is a man with a great desire for children.

Papi doesn't trust him and has told Mami more than once not to leave me alone with him, but she doesn't care so she calls him when Papi is not there, to ask him to help me. She is silly. I write to her that I don't want to see him, but she takes my spirit notebook away and will not give it to me unless I speak. My spirit notebook has been blessed by Aura. She's passed it through the smoke of the frankincense and blessed it with her prayers.

I gesture with my hands for her to give it to me. She makes a gesture to smack me with it, but I move away. She begins to read what I wrote *El ojo desnudo ha perdido sus alas.*

"Why can't you say what you mean, Mia? Why do you speak like this?"

"It's the dead," I say, and I hear my voice.

She's startled by it, too, but the doorbell rings and she jumps.

I go to my room. She speaks to the doctor, "I just heard her speak," she says, to him. "Something about the dead. Can she speak to them?" Then she whispers something, but all I hear is "like the mother."

El Doctor tries to calm her down and then I hear his footsteps, reminding me of the rustling tail of the Devil in my dreams.

"Are you ok?" he asks.

I don't answer him. I know that he's a doctor who opens women's legs and check their privates. I remain quiet and look away.

I know, he'll open me up and check my private parts and tell me stories, recover the memories written on my body.

"I'm not going to hurt you," he says as if I am going to believe him.

I sit on the windowsill near the fire escape. I press my legs close together so he won't get any ideas. He comes towards me; his warm hand rests on my lap. It's a large hand and it trembles while it touches me, waiting to see what I will do. I don't move. I don't resist, but I look at him straight in the eyes, and I see something I don't want to see. I see sorrow, I see pain, and I see regret. I hold my prayer pouch, the one Aura made for my protection, and I have my talking board on my lap. He looks at both.

"Maybe you can help me," he says. "Maybe you can pray for me. Aura says that your prayers are very powerful."

My heart is racing fast as I feel his hand there on my lap. His hands are shaking; his forehead is teary with sweat. I hope he has not taken Aura's heart.

"Maybe I can't," I say and take his tarantula hand away from my leg.

"I'm sure you can,"

He comes close to me, so close I can smell the lemon scent of his cologne, and he kisses my forehead. Then he looks into my eyes. Maybe he doesn't like what he sees there because he leaves quickly, passing my mother without saying good-bye.

Mami comes to the room, her forehead wrinkled, smelling of fish stew.

"What did you do to the Doctor?" my mother asks while drying her hands on her green apron. I do not speak. She stares at me and the talking board on my lap.

I don't look at her either because it's disrespectful; I just lower my eyes and look at my protection pouch. She walks back to her kitchen duties.

Papi is entering the apartment and he sees *el Doctor* walking out.

"Why was he here?"

"I asked him."

"Why?"

"It doesn't matter. She did something to *el Doctor* and he ran out of here,"

"Mia, did something to him?" Papi questions her.

"*Sí*, Mia,"

"What have I told you,"

My father is mad. There is a silence. My mother sighs.
"Is not true, Suarez, he's not that kind of man. She did
something to him with the Ouija board and ...," Mami is
speechless.

"I don't want that man near my daughter, do you
understand?" he screams.

I smile.

My joy is returning. It returns in this little light in my
heart that seems to glow like a flame, letting me know that
the world is not totally lopsided and messed up.

The Journey

I don't hang out with Mimi and Rosa anymore. I go more
and more to la Botánica to hang out with Aura, or I help her
at home with her spiritual cleansing potions. Today, Aura
cleanses her apartment with the clapping of her hands to all
four heavenly corners and the sprinkles of *Agua de Florida*
to bring healing spirits my way. On an incense pot she places
coal, lights it up, and blows on it until it is red-hot. Once it's
lit, she places tiny pebbles of frankincense and they begin to
turn yellow and brown. They melt, and as they do, the sweet
smoke begins to rise, and it reminds me of a church, of a
holy place where only good things happen.

Aura honors the winds by blowing it to the South, the
North, the East and the West. She cleanses me by passing the
incense around me, "*Para tu cuerpo, túuespíritu, tu mente y
tus emociones,*" for my body, spirit, mind, and in front of my
heart for my emotions. I sit in lotus pose just like Aura's
Buddha on the altar.

"Find your breath," Aura says. "Take a deep breath to
relax the mind."

I do, inhaling the sweet aroma of the incense and raising my hands to honor my ancestors and God.

"You are going on a journey and breath is everything," she adds.

I breathe again.

"Clear your eyes, Mia," and I close them.

"Yes, relax and take deep breaths," and I do.

"Look at the images in your mind..."

Aura's warm hands touch my shoulder, and her warmth passes like a current through my body. Sitting now on the sacred space, the healing blanket, I close my eyes and let the images float before me. "Let the images pass you by, let them float...let them tell you a story...good."

I begin to see water. Warm and blue. The green mountains, large, their scent of night...the sunrises and sunsets.... I fly above this beautiful place. I see an island, the island of my birth, but I have no memories of it. I have never been there, yet the place is familiar. It is warm and the waters are blue green, and the air has flowery, sweet scent. I feel at peace. I go down and land there. The grass is cool, and the air smells like mangoes and pineapples, I feel safe. I hear sounds, music and drums, and hear singing. I see a path. It is like a garden. It is like Eden. I walk to find a sacred circle of dark people with straight long hair. They are dancing to the rhythm of the drums. They are half-naked, and I tell Aura. "The women wear *enaguas*. They are dancing, celebrating; they are happy. I feel like I am home...safe...home... I follow a path... I reach a center, a circle. I am surrounded by peace."

"Good, you've reached the sacred center, *el centro de la tranquilidad, ve ahi.*"

"They greet me as if they expected me. I go...a woman takes my hand and I follow her. She's laughing. I feel like I am floating."

"If you float or travel up, you are in the upper world, the heavens. In the heavens you find your teacher, your guides, and your angels. They have something to teach you. Listen."

"Now, I come down and I am running with this beautiful Taína."

"Ok, then you are in the present world, the world of your now. In this world you will see your present."

"Yes, I see my father, I see myself as a child when my father loved me. I see Mami, and las Tías, and they are waving at me. Zuki, Mimi, Rosa and other cousins. I see Pito. I see… memories of the things I want to forget."

"Honra esa memoria," she tells me. "Bless these memories. They are there to teach you something."

I bless them and move on. In my memories I do not fear my father, but love him. In my memories, I am not lonely but belong to my family. I am sad now. Pain. Sadness. The present. Pito. Eva. Rica. Zuleika. The beating. The memories, they flow through my body, the body that remembers everything. I allow it. I see the past. The past when my father loved me. I see me when I was as a child, loving my father and loving my family.

"I'm floating …."

"Let it be. You are going to the heavens to meet your guide."

I fly up to the heavens and I see fluffy clouds.

"Listen to your spiritual guide."

I find it. It is a being that I cannot see but is. I hear it, but I do not see it. It says, *"Roco, Roco, Roco,"* and I know that this word means to know, but I do not know how I know. I hear *"Tureyo, Tureyo, Turey,"* and I know it means the sky…the voice of the sky… and I follow it, but everything happens quickly. It says to know the sky, to follow the sky.

"I'm falling now. Everything happens quickly…I follow, but then I fall quickly, down through a cloud, soft and fluffy it takes me to the ground, to present earth, but then I'm in front of a cave."

"You are now in the underworld. If you see yourself entering holes, or falling, you are in the underworld. Enter the cave. There are gifts there."

I enter the dark cave. It smells like sweet morning rain, the scent of earth and water, hibiscus, jasmine, the sweet scent calling me. I enter the cave and fall deeper, and when I land, a sweet turtle appears to me. She smells like the sweet waters of rivers and she's so beautiful and strong. The turtle comes out of its shell. She smiles and I am warmed by her kindness. 'Do you understand memory?' the turtle asks me."

"Good," Aura says, "Good. When one is given the space to let go of a memory, it no longer has power, Mia. She wants to know that you know."

I think of my memory and I suddenly understand what happened, us playing hooky, Eva's fear and her lies, my father's beating. I suddenly understand. The turtle says it was not my fault. She smiles at me, her wrinkled little neck moving to one side. I want to take her with me. Aura says you can do a lot with memories—you can bury them in your body, you can bury them in your mind and forget them, you can nurture them with understanding, or put them away by forgiving them. "Memories can be put to rest by giving them away, by giving them a voice," the turtle says and then I am not sure if Aura is the turtle or the turtle is Aura, but their voices are the same.

I compose myself. I take a deep breath and dry my tears. We come full circle. Aura and I clean up the living room area, thanking God and our ancestors, clapping to the four winds, and sprinkling *Agua de Florida*.

When we finish cleaning, Aura begins to cook. She takes Yuca out of the refrigerator and she blesses it.

"The food of our ancestors," she says and I laugh.

As she cooks she tells me a story of our ancestors, los indios Taínos. "According to our myths, in the beginning there was Yaya. Yaya was everything, the father, the spirit, the beginning. Everything was going fine, but Yaya's son, Yayael, was going through a tough adolescence and giving Yaya a hard time. Yayael was rebelling, and his father, out of fear that Yayael would take his place, killed him and put his bones in a *Calabaza*, a pumpkin and hung it up on the roof of his *Bohio*, his hut. I am sure Yaya prayed for his son and was sad for having lost his temper and hurting him in such a way."

I cuddle on the sofa while I listen to Aura who starts to sauté onions and fries Salchichon for dinner. I watch as she pours the tomato sauce.

"At the same time," she says "Itiba Cahuaba, the giver of life was giving birth to four children twins. The first to come is Caracaracol; his skin was hard like a shell, so they called him that. Then she gave birth to Deminan, and then the other two came along. The father was Yucahu Bagua Maorocoti, the being of the Yuca, the soul who is of the sky, whom no one can see, and I think you met Yucahu, up in the sky. It was Yucahu who told you to know the sky."

"Yes. The heavens, but go on."

"So, the four divine twins are created between mother earth and father sky. It is said that Yucahu was represented in the *Cemies*, these little rocks that have three points, like that one I found in our backyard in Santo Domingo."
I look at her little altar next to the window, and I get up to look at the *Cemies*, a being made like a triangle of rock.

"Interesting," I say. She continues.

"They were often buried in the land for fertility of crops, usually corn and yuca, these were the special foods of the Taíno Indians. One day, when Yaya wasn't home, the four divine twins, Itiba, Cahubaby, Deminan and Caracaracol dislodged the magical pumpkin from the roof of his house where the bones of his son Yayael where buried and where fish and water had been born, and suddenly all of the fish poured out, and they began to eat them, but they heard that Yaya was coming back and tried to put it all back, but they couldn't do it right, that is putting the calabaza back up, and it fell and broke, and all of the waters of the pumpkin filled the earth and from there came all the fish, and they say that this is how the ocean originated. They ran out and ended up in their grandfather's house, Bayamanaco, the God of Fire, and he guarded the making of *Cazabe*, the delicious bread we make from Yuca and the *Cohoba*, a drink that was used to call up images during their religious rituals, which allowed the Taíno Indians to communicate with their Gods, and so Deminan took the initiative and asked Bayamanaco for some *Cazabe* and Bayamanaco was so angry he spat fire at Deminan's back, a *Guanguayo*, a spit of the brew of *Cohoba* he made that morning, and he ran out, but when he met his brothers and they saw what happened to his back, they realized that he suddenly had a hunchback, and the hunchback grew until he almost died, and so the brothers opened the back from where a female turtle, Caguama, came out. She is the mother of humans who came into being from the back of Demian."

"So I met Caguama?"

"Yes, you did."

"What do you think she was she trying to say to me?"

"What do you think? You went on this long journey, so it's up to you to find out."

"I guess she's trying to tell me to get out of my shell," I laugh.

"That's sounds good."

"She wants me to find my voice, to be strong, to not give in. To never give up. She wants me to know that things grow slowly…to take my time."

"Wait," she says to me, "I almost forgot," and she runs to her purse.

"Here," she says, and gives me a bag. I open it.

"I found it today," she says, out of breath.

Inside was a sculpted little turtle made of our of a smooth green rock. There it stood, a gift to remind me.

Hello, My Sky

Papi comes to my bed and sits next to me. "*Hola, mi cielo,*" he says, calling me his sky. As a child I liked it when he said things like that, or when he said that I was his other half. I look at him and my voice returns.

"Hola, Papi."

My father is pleased, but doesn't make a scene. He hugs me and says, "Tío Quinto wants to come over after dinner." He coughs, "For a family prayer."

I stay quiet. My uncle Tío Quinto wants to undo what he's done. He wants to bring healing to the family. He feels everything and everyone is out of balance because since the beating nothing has been the same and he worries about the future.

"Eva will come too. It's time for you to talk to each other. I think she needs you," Papi says.

I am sure that Tío is hoping that Papi will take away my Talking Board, my spirit notebook, and I worry. I have the board on my bed, and I hold it.

"It's ok, you can keep it," Papi says, "It's just a family prayer." He touches my hand, the hand that is touching the Ouija Board, "You don't have to do it," Papi says, "but I think it will help us all," and he tells me he never meant to hurt me in the ways he hurt me; neither did Tío Quinto. I swallow hard, and a desire to cry is so profound in me that I feel the tears swimming in my throat and I feel them swelling in my eyes.

"Yes," I say, and I imagine my uncle with his bible in his hand, asking for God's guidance, and the women in the background like a choir, saying "*Alabado sea el señor.*" I imagine *la Guela* sprinkling *Agua de Florida* all over the room, and Aura, the one who knows the mysteries, praying with her eyes closed, and I sit on the bed and hug my father, "*Sí,* Papi, *sí.*"

He kisses my forehead where I have a third eye that sees

everything. When Papi leaves, the scent of his woody fragrance is everywhere, on my sheets, on my hands, on my body, even on my third eye. When he's gone, I breathe the scent of him left in the palm of my hand. I inhale his love into me. In and out I take my father, and he becomes a butterfly.

Aura

Aura was one of those women who was not family, but was family, and no one knew how. It took some time for me to put all of the pieces of the puzzle together and find the truth about Aura, but by then, she'd be gone due to breast cancer like most of the women in my family. My aunt, Tati says that Aura's mother, Nene, was a spiritist, a psychic, a prostitute and my maternal grandfather's mistress. On his death bed, my mother had promised him that she'd take care of his mistress if he died, and she did. I am sure it was not easy, but my mother is generous like that. She made sure Nene came to New York in the 60's when everyone had to leave after the overthrow of Trujillo, something the family never spoke of.

My family was like a book without previous chapters. They held the past at bay, kept it secret from us. Illness was another one of those secrets too. When Nene died of breast cancer. A secret. When Aura died, another secret. I wonder if I too will hold secrets from my daughter when she's grown, if I too hold the legacy of shame and silence, or if I will free myself of my past and share these secrets with her, but she is too young for me to tell her such things now. I keep these stories to myself, telling her only in small doses. When she finds Aura's photo, I don't know what to say. A family friend. A dear loved one.

Aura never told us how old she was, but I could tell by the lines that form under her eyes when she laughed. The thin lines appearing on the edge of her eyes like chicken legs were evidence of her wisdom, she said, and not age. She wore a blob of blue eye shadow over her dark eyelids and heavy makeup in order to hide holes from her chicken pox. I imagine that she was older than she said she was. She laughed a lot. She'd say what was the point of living if your face didn't show that your past had had a history full of love and joy. She acted young, though, like one of the Hippies in the street, like a flower child. She wore flowing skirts from India and

Maxi dresses with *lentejuelas* that glittered when she moved around. She wore an ankle bracelet with bells that rang when she walked. She was not a young person, nor an old one, yet she could hang out with us young people, and she could be a consultant to the elders. She was ageless. Short and dark with straight black hair that reached her waist. She was a mystery.

I never saw Aura take a bath, but she always smelled sweet like a crushed flower in an old book. Something about her was old and comforting. Rosa and Mimi fought for who would sleep in her house at night. They liked the lavender scent of her bed, the roses on her table, the frankincense she'd burn when she prayed and the scent of mature fruit, offerings to the saints.

During the day, Aura worked in la Botánica, Yemaya, a spiritual store on Jerome Avenue. Her mother, Nene, worked there with her. A psychic by nature, Nene supported herself with the power of her seeing. She'd read *Las Barajas Españolas* and cleansed homes possessed by restless spirits. Aura had her gift, and, according to them, I was following their footsteps. "It seems to run in the blood," Aura said. This seemed to make them proud. Like her mother, Aura read the tarot cards; cleansed homes of people in distress, and cured the sick with the palm of her hand. Papi let me go to her Botánica and do my homework there after school, and I would help Aura clean up and organize all of the powders and potions in alphabetical order. Every day was a special event at la Botánica. Monday was the day of Abundance; Tuesday the Day of Victory; Wednesday the Day of Confusion; Thursday, the Day of Marriage; Friday the Day of Trouble; Saturday the Day of Evil Resolutions; and Sunday the Day of Tranquility, each day guided by a Yoruba Deity and a Catholic Saint, each day with its special ritual and prayer. Aura made sure that we learned about life and death, about spirits and their special guidance, about honoring our ancestors after their passing.

"That side," she'd say, "It's as special and real as this side."

She had the knowledge given to her by her mother and her mother's elders, all of whom knew of the mysteries, *eso mysterios* that she was teaching us day by day.

And my family, no matter how religious they were, believed in her, trusted her. The truth was that as long as there were no boys involved in our supposed childlike rituals, the family would let us raise the dead and more. Boys were dangerous. The dead were dead. But that All Hallows Eve of 1972 would end up being a magical and memorable day. Aura said that with the power of our prayer and our beliefs, we would rid a man of an evil spirit that haunted his days and nights and made him want to do things with children no one was allowed to do. Aura told us old tales of the Zangano, a spirit who possess a person and made them want to hurt children sexually. Aura had asked us to help her with a spiritual cleansing of this Zangano spirit and so we had promised to help her because it was *el Doctor* who was possessed and he was like family, she said.

"God will heal him through us," Aura said, "and he will be cleansed and your future will be safe."

That night, I opened an eye and Tati asked me to close it. She was applying makeup on my eyes for Halloween, the only time my cousins and I were allowed to wear it.

"You girls are taking this too seriously," Tati said, and Zuki and I giggled.

"It's just Halloween," Zuki said, and I blinked as Tati applied the makeup.

"*Sí*... pero...," she said and went on to say that there was something mysterious in the air. Tati was one of those mothers who could sense the energy of something changing, and she knew there was too much intensity in our supposed childlike game of witches.

"*Ay, Mami, por favor,*" Zuki said. I liked how Zuki would

answer her mother. I would never dare talk to my mother like that.

"Ya," Tati said, saying she'd finished my makeup, and I could check my eyes out in the mirror. I did, and I liked what I saw—a girl growing and becoming . Tati echoed what I longed to hear from my own mother, "You look beautiful."

Zuki and I wore amber earrings and necklaces. We topped off our beautiful velvet long dresses with the black-hooded Tabards that Tía had sown for us. The dresses reached down to the floor. I put on some Sabbath oil made by Aura and chanted with my eyes closed. I could hear Tia's laughter at our childlike antics, "Have fun," Tía said as she kissed our foreheads and gave us blessing and sent us with God.

As we left, we found Rosa and Mimi on the second floor. We hugged and screamed and twirled in the hallway, squealing like adolescents tend to do.

"Are you ready?, " Rosa asked Zuki.

"We'll do fine," I said, when Mimi chimed in: "I remember my words, do you?"

"Yes, I do," I said.

"I'm always ready," Mimi said, and she pointed out that she wouldn't let us do anything to hurt *el Doctor* who was coming as honored guest for cleansing.

"It's not about hurting, it's about cleansing,"

"Does Rica know?" Mimi asked. Our friend, Rica, was his daugther. We wondered for a moment if he ever touched Rica in the ways he touch Rosa and Mili. Rica never spoke about it.

"Who cares," Rosa said. "He wants to get better."

"How do you know?" Mimi asked and Rosa pointed out how he was letting us do this cleansing so that he could get well and never hurt children ever again. "He wants to get better," Mimi said.

I had to admit, he had never touched me, although I could

feel the desire in his eyes, but he never did anything. Aura said that a man who has the Zangano spirit in him will always have this desire, but if you cleanse the Zangano out of him, he'd be free.

"I'll erase his memories," I said, and the girls looked at me as we went up the stairs to Aura's apartment.

"Memories?"

"Maybe his hurting children has to do with bad memories... I don't know... maybe memories make people hurt other people."

"Not all memories make people hurt other people. Sometimes, memories make you stop from hurting them, that's what Aura said," Zuki told us.

"If he doesn't have the memory, maybe he doesn't have to worry," Rosa said.

"Aura says that memories need to be understood not erased," Zuki said.

Rosa teased Mimi, "Let's erase his memories completely, and then he can't even remember who he is,"

"Stop it," Mimi said, reminding Rosa of her psychic dyslexia. Rosa couldn't do magic at all. If she prayed for sun, it snowed. If she prayed for peace, a fight ensued.

"Our motto is do no harm, remember?" I said, so let's stop this silly talk about what we will or will not do.

"I'll shrink his ass," Rosa said "I'll make his thing a little thing," she added as she showed us with her fingers how tiny she planned to make it. I laughed at the thought, for I had never seen the thing anyway to have any idea of why Rosa wanted to shrink it.

"Stop it," Mimi said. "You can't do that, we're trying to help him, we're taking out the evil spirit, Rosa," Mimi added.

"Yes, we are. It's All Hallows Eve, the day when magic happens," I said.

We finally arrived at Aura's apartment, our mouths dry from talking about our plans against *el Doctor*. We stood in front of the door and it opened slowly like magic.

"Enter into my kingdom of lightness," Aura said.

Her whole being flickered like a candle, and we entered hypnotized by her presence. The scent of herbs, musk and incense permeated the air. We entered quickly and sat in a meditating position to do our breathing exercises, and we looked at our candle for guidance. Then she went and escorted our blind folded doctor into the room.

"*¿De dónde vienes?*" she asked him.

"Where do you come from?" we echoed.

"*Yo vengo del sur...,*" he coughed as if he had forgotten his lines, and then he repeated in English.

"I come from the South, where there are sweet rivers."

We echoed his words and Zuki hit the chimes.

"*Yo vengo del sitio más oscuro,*" he added, and asked for help. "Y vengo en busca *de* ayuda."

"¿Para donde vas?" she asked.

"Where do you go?" we repeated.

"I go to the North in search of the light, to show me the way" he said in Spanish.

"I, the guardian of the Bronx light tower of the North, forbid you entrance until you are purified. Whom do you trust?"

"I trust God."

"What is the password?"

"I believe in Karma, that what goes around comes around."

"What is your mission?"

"To do no harm," he said.

"Son of God, approach me, the mother guardian of the light tower, and receive my blessing of life on earth."

Aura sprinkled salt on to his forehead and then passed her hands around him. Around her hands a flow moved and then it seemed as if it was pulling something out of him.

Then I noticed a green color coming out of him, out it flowed, and then resisted and re-entered him. Then it came out and in again until she had total control of the green slime and put it in the *caldero* that she had in front of her. *El Doctor* took deep breaths in and out for ten times, and then he seemed to be released. There was a smile on his face. He was cleansed.

"Bless you mother-guardian of the light tower" he said. "I shall be cleansed and the spirits within me shall leave me and go where there is end,"

"Listen to me, once a month when the moon is full, we shall meet in this place of light, and I shall bring healing to your soul. Let me bless you with the five-folded kiss so that I may grant you entrance into our kingdom, and you shall do no harm." Then Aura moved to bestow the five-folded kiss.

"I bless your lips that have uttered the sacred oath," and Aura kissed his lips, lightly and suddenly.

"I bless you breast that are formed in beauty and in strength" and Aura kissed his breast.

Aura knelt before this big man, her hair flowing on the floor. Her body covered by her velvet tabard. She knelt before him and said, "I bless your feet that bought you here," and she kissed his feet. "I bless your knees that shall kneel at the holy altar," and she kissed his knees.

"I bless thy organ of generation without which we would not be," she said and added, "Will you be true to the mysteries of the spirit?" and we girls rang the bell seven times each and then Aura asked again "will you be true to the mysteries of the spirit?"

"I shall be true to the mysteries of the spirit."

The following week the store windows on 170th St. in the Bronx took down all of their decorations of pumpkins and witches on broomsticks and replaced them with turkeys and pilgrims. Autumn had arrived, and with it the winds of change. It was 1972, and my brother Charlie was going to college and not to war, and Papi was planning the move from the Bronx back to Santo Domingo, his dream.

In the corner of 170ᵗʰ Street, we found *el Doctor*, handing out religious pamphlets from one of local churches, *El Ricón de Dios*. He had a large loudspeaker and asked everyone to repent and find Jesus. People passed by him and took his handouts or stood before him to listen. He was charismatic and looked like a Latino Clark Gable. The women smiled and asked about the church that he urged them to attend. When I passed by him *el Doctor* did not remember our childlike game of witches. No memory at all. I wondered, too, if he remembered his past. I thought memory was to be understood and not erased, but Aura said that sometimes, so it happens, one begins anew. I understood then why she wanted to heal *el Doctor*, I think she wanted to protect us, to protect other women, or maybe she felt sorry for him.

A week later, I found Aura outside sitting on the stoops of the steps. It was a gorgeous Autumn day, clear and cool, and the scent of burning leaves arrived at the Bronx from heaven knows where. My parents were moving back to the Dominican Republic. Papi had a good job with the government. We already had a house.

"I'm leaving" I said to her.

"I know,"

"I'll miss you," I said to her, my throat was tight.

She placed her long bangs behind her ears, and I noticed how pretty she'd colored her eyelids, all blue like the sky, making her dark eyes more mysterious.

"Will you remember me, Mia?" she asked.

"Always."

"Where do you go?" she asked, as in one of our rituals. I laughed. She stood before me and she looked at me. Her eyes were luminous, but held a certain sadness.

"I go to the South where the waters are warm, and the sun is bright, I go in search of the light, to show me the way."

"What is the password?" She asked

"I believe in Karma, that what goes around comes around."

"What is your mission?" she said, acting serious, but with a smile.

To do no harm."

"I, the guardian of the Bronx light tower of the North, forbid you entrance until you are purified. Whom do you trust?"

"I trust God," I said, and she came towards me and held me close and very, very tight.

The Time Keeper

Mia walked towards her father, stood behind him, and covered his eyes with her sweaty hands. She kissed his bald head as he sat on floral wing chair reading *el Listín Diario*. Every night, he read every newspaper, but he left her the *Listín Diario* because Mia would cut out poetry and literary pieces. She'd cut them and paste them in her journal. From the other newspapers she would cut out *Amor Es*, by an American artist name Kim. Mia would also cut out *el Pozo de la Dicha*, a box with numbers whose message would be deciphered by adding the letters of her name and coming up with a key number that would give her a daily message in one word—for example, *Felicidad*. She was not, however, allowed to cut anything related to death or political events.

It was Christmas in 1972 and she was living in Santo Domingo for the first time since she had left after the overthrow of the Dominican dictator, Trujillo. *Navidades* in Santo Domingo were not like in New York City. In Santo Domingo, *Navidades* was a lively time that started in the early weeks of December and didn't end until Three Kings Day on January 6. Everyone Mia knew was roaming house to house *en Trullas* singing *Aguinaldos*, and looking forward to *La Misa del Gallo on Noche Buena*, but her father was too strict to let her attend a midnight mass on Christmas Eve. Her father didn't believe Mia should be out at midnight gallivanting around with boys and girls, even if it was a church, but Mia was in love with a boy name Miguel Angel and this party and a walk to *la Misa del Gallo* would solidify their relationship and make it plain for everyone to see that Mia was going steady with him, *teniendo amores*, like people there were known to say.

Her father peeled himself from the *Listín Diario*, his forehead sweaty and his eyes red, and telling Mia that she was an egg. Mia could tell if it was a politically bad day because her father's forehead would grow damp and red. Her father never spoke about his job, but she knew that he worked for Joaquin Balaguer, the President, but she didn't know what he did. All of the men in the family worked for the government. She knew that there were things you could not do or say and that her father seemed more worried now then when they were in the United States. People were dying or disappearing, men were fighting for causes, reporters were killed for speaking their thoughts, young adults in the university rioted against the government, and youth were easily deported to Russia for their beliefs. Questions were not allowed in her family, and her life was to be a continuous stream of denial. She did not feel fear, but believed the world was safe, although she was not allowed to walk around unchaperoned, a guard stood at the front of her house and a chauffer or her father escorted her to most events. In the evening, when she slept she could hear her father's whispered conversations with her mother, "Things never change." At night, he'd sulk and not sleep, and during the day he protected Mia from the reality she herself tried to deny.

"Never be a reporter or politician," he'd say to her, but wouldn't explain that in a world where truth had to be denied, the written word could cause your death. "Never marry a politician," he'd say, and she wished for once that he'd explain what he meant, but he wouldn't. To him, she was a just a child, and children needed to be protected from the truth. He wanted her to live an idyllic youth, believing the world was good, and only in those moments of loss and sadness would he share with her a minimal truth. So when Mia came and stood before him, he could sense her presence by the scent of her sweet flowery fragrance, her soft hands covering his eyes, the eyes that could not see that she was growing to be a young woman with ideas of her own, his heart skipped a beat for a moment, and he stood there until he was awakened by her warm lips on his bald head.

"Ese huevo quiere sal," he said that Mia was an egg, and

she wanted salt—an old saying, which meant that she was only being loving, and kind to get what she wanted, which was true. Her father looked at his watch to check the time and then looked at her.

"Papi, I'm not an egg," she said laughing, as she sat next to him and cuddled against him. She took in his scent Vetiver and felt the warmth of his body.

"But you're acting like an egg."

"Well, it's just that…"

"Admit it," he said, "You're an old egg."

She laughed, "Yes, yes, I'm an egg, and I want a lot of salt," and then she asked him in the sweetest voice he could to let her attend the midnight mass, but she didn't tell him that this mass was like an engagement, which would solidify her relationship with Miguel Angel.

"I hope this party is not over that boy, Miguel Angel."

Miguel Angel was a seventeen year old senior at a private high school for boys. His family was not religious, but followed the Order of the Rose and the Cross, the Rosicrucians. They were a mysterious esoteric group that believed in the mysteries very much like the spiritual traditions of some of her family members like her cousin Aura, who could heal with her hands and tell a person destiny with numerology or Tarot cards. Mia was fascinated. Miguel Angel's father was, however, a member of the Dominican Revolutionary Party. Her father, who worked for the President, the opposite.

"I don't think your father would like me," he often said, but so far her father didn't like anyone. He suspected every boy of being a communist, a sexual perpetrator or a drug addict. As her father confronted her with his suspicions, she stood beside him trying to control her nerves. Her hands trembled and her lips quivered as she lied.

"No, Papi, no,"

"Esa familia es rara," he said, that the family was weird and he went on, *"dizque rosa cruces, comunista, vagabundo"*

he added and went on to discredit the family and their political beliefs.

"Ay, Papi, for you everyone is a communist," she laughed. Despite her father's talk, he was a caring man who consistently cared for the poor and instilled in her a deep commitment to serving others, particularly those in need. Yet, he had a terrible fear of communism. He was afraid that the Dominican Republic was in jeopardy of becoming another Cuba.

"*La Misa del Gallo*, is a community event, in a church, with friends and their parents."

He looked at her in silence. Mia knew that her father was a spiritual man, who honored his ancestors with candles, prayers and food offerings, but never went to church.

"I don't know, Mia. It's kind of late." her father said, reminding her of her ten o'clock curfew and that there was no chauffer to take her and that he didn't like her out all by herself at night.

"Cinderella had a midnight curfew, Papi."

"You're not Cinderella."

"For just that reason, let me go to the mass and I'll be back right after it."

"What time is the party?"

"Ten."

"Ten," he repeated.

"Yes."

"It's too late, Mia."

Her father was the ultimate timekeeper. He believed there was a time for everything—a time to wake up, a time to eat, a time to go to bed, a time to study, a time to rest and most of all a time to love, and her time, he reminded her, had not come. For this reason, he didn't think Mia should be en *el Muro de la Jamona*, talking to boys or walking unsupervised to the main grocery store, *el colmado* Rocky Bear's where everyone bought their daily bread, and local gossip, but Mia was in love with the most amazing boy and she needed to go to this mass.

"There will be a lot of supervision," Mia said pressing her case. "It's a street party, Papi. Everyone will be there."

She mentioned the daughter of *el Doctor* Suazo the owner of the pharmacy on Pisces Street, was allowing his daughter to attend. In addition, the daughter of *el Lincenciado* Villanueva who lived on Sagitario Street in that big old white house would be there too. She name dropped, *un doctor o ingeniero* here and a *lincenciado* there. He hesitated, lowered the newspaper and asked a few more questions. Then he sighed. "Well, you can attend the party, but you must be back by eleven,"

"Eleven."

"Yes."

"Papi, that's just one hour."

"That's it."

"But, I won't be able to go to the midnight mass."

"Twelve then and no church."

"No, church, Papi, then what's the point?" she said, knowing that he needed to assert his authority, but what family would not allow a daughter to attend church?

He draped himself with his *Listín Diario* again and remained quiet.

"Church is the most important part of the event Papi. Come with me then, come and supervise me, if this is the problem," she said, and he looked hurt.

"What about your mother?" he said and placed the newspaper on his lap.

Her mother had been sick, but she couldn't remember a time when her mother wasn't sick.

"Julia will take care of her," she said. Julia was the housekeeper who cared for all of them as if they were her own family. She supervised her mother's every breath.

"You are so selfish, Mia."

She lowered her eyes in shame.

"A person has a choice," he said, "to accept or deny the choice given. You can go, but have to be back by midnight; if not, don't go," he said and waited for a thanks filled with enthusiasm, but Mia just stared at him and walked away. Her father was insufferable, she thought. How could he keep her locked up in this tower like a child held inside a clock, suspended in time.

The days passed slowly, idyllically. At night she read about the Rosicrucians in a booklet Miguel Angel had given her. On Friday, she went to *El Paseo de Los Indios* for a walk with her friends, and at night she lay with her mother and watched the Spanish soap operas. Before she went to bed, she prayed, summarized the day's events in her journals or cut up literary pieces from *El Listen* for future use. On nights she couldn't sleep, she'd read Freud's *Interpretation of Dreams*, a book she had found in her uncle's library. He had a large two-story house with an observatory because he was an amateur astronomer and he had the largest library she had ever seen. She discovered that dreams were a source of guidance, for often when she wrote them down and tried to understand them, she learned that they were telling her how to proceed or to be careful in various situations.

The night before the party Mia was restless. How would she be able to convince her father to let her go to church? She put Freud's book under her pillow and asked Freud if he could give her the answers in her dream. The first night nothing happened, but he second night the gift came. Mia slept and dreamt of Freud. She was in his office, there was a couch, all leather and luscious, and many clocks ticking. The room was dark, like an old sepia photo, and he stared at her in that inquisitive way she had seen in photos in her uncle's library. Some of the clocks had women's faces and wings. There were clocks going backwards in time and grandfather clocks with the shape of women. She stared at them. Their hands were real hands with fingers pointing at the time, and that frightened her, but Freud smiled at her and motioned for her to sit on the couch and then he said, *"Dime la historia del tiempo,"* tell me the history of time, and she told him about what she wanted, and then he asked her to look at the palm of her hand where the face of a clock appeared, and the hands of the clock were moving backwards.

When Mia woke up she could not understand the dream. She wrote the images in her journal and doodled thoughts about each image. She looked at the palm of her hand, and she wrote, "taking matters into her own hands," and she liked that, and then there was the clock going backwards, and she thought of time. Did backwards mean her childhood, or her father' antiquated ways of thinking? Maybe. Hands. The clock was printed on her hands, and the hands of the clock were going back, back in time. She walked around the house and looked at all of the clocks and finally the answer appeared. Freud was telling her to change the clocks in the house, to take matters into her own hands, by moving the hands of the clock back by an hour or two. She laughed and laughed. She would take life into her own hands and change the hands of all the clocks in the house to give her enough time to go to *la Misa del Gallo*.

On that night before leaving, Mia changed all of the clocks by one hour. Julia, the housekeeper, caught her and helped her change the remaining clocks, starting with the kitchen, and then the living room, and they went from room to room until each clock allowed her one extra hour and a half. When it was twelve on her watch, she'd be in la *Misa del Gallo* with Miguel Angel and at home it would be earlier Her father would not worry. He would not even notice. She'd stay only half an hour at the *Misa* and run back home. Her parents would be asleep and unaware of the change.

On the night of *La Misa del Gallo*, Rica picked her up along with her twenty-two-year old boyfriend, Estanly. They caught up with Miguel Angel who was waiting for them at *el Muro de la Jamona*. He looked great with bell-bottom beige pants and a psychedelic polyester shirt. She felt proud to be with him. She found him attractive, confident and mature. He had strong features, large eyes with bushy eyebrows that connected, and a square smooth chin. She loved his hair, it was straight, light brown, long, and loose, and, unlike her hair, it never frizzed in the heat or humidity. Her hair grew wild, and she often pushed it back in a bun out of shame in a country where curly hair was not acceptable. When he saw her, he combed his long hair back with his fingers. She knew his father must be furious because it was considered rebellious in the Dominican Republic for a young man to have long hair. Long hair to her father meant you were either a drug addict or a communist.

La Misa del Gallo was a big occasion in the Jardines Zodiacales. There were tables and chairs and music and children running all around the place. Mia was nervous about being in such a large group of people, about changing the clocks, about being in love, but she greeted others with calm. She settled in a semi-secluded part of the Plaza to talk to Miguel Angel. Estanly, the local disc jockey, set the music for the night, and they prayed that the power wouldn't go off as it often did. However, an *apagón*, as they called the brief blackouts in Santo Domingo, would give time for a kiss without the watchful eyes of the elders.

The scented night air smelled sweet. It was a wild plant the boys called a whore by night and a virgin by day. It would open up at night and exude a sweet scent and then sleep all day when the light hit it. A *bolero* came on, *Reloj No Marques Las Horas* by Lucho Gatica. As a child she would dance to this with her father, her small feet on top of his large shinny shoes. She felt like a lady when she did that. The song started, *Reloj no marques las horas, porque voy a enloquecer, ella se irá para siempre, cuando amanezca otra vez.* The song was a request for time to stand still because she, the loved one, would leave when the sun rose.

Everyone started to dance, and Miguel Angel took her hand and lead her to the center of the plaza. Mia heard the words of the song and she started to laugh as she interpreted the lyrics that said that the loved one only had this night to live their love, and the tick-tock of the clock reminded him of his pain.

"Do you believe in coincidences?" she asked him.

"I do," he said. "Why?"

"Sometimes you wish for something and it appears. I like those kinds of coincidences. It's like the world is filled with magic, and these little coincidences are a reminder that the world was full of miracles," she said.

The song continued, reminding her of its message. The woman in the song was the star that brightens the man's world; without her he felt life was nothing because as time passed she was moving on, and he was begging the clock to hold time still. He did not want things to change.

"I know what you mean."

"This song, for example, it's my father's favorite song."

"And?" he said as he held her close.

"As a child, I'd stand on Papi's shoes and dance boleros," she said as she looked down at his feet. He laughed.

"I loved my father so much as a child. I still do, please don't get me wrong."

"I know."

"It's just that now that my mom is sick, whenever she's feeling better, my father dances this song with her," Mia said. "There is something sad when they dance, like they don't want to lose each other, or like they know they will. It seems hard for him to deal with this," and she thought of the lyrics, the request for time to stand still, to hold his hands and allow the night to be perpetual because he doesn't want her to leave him ever, and he doesn't want the sun to rise without her.

"So there is this song, time, your father, and coincidences. What are you trying to say?"

"I can't go to *la Misa del Gallo*. Papi wouldn't let me."

"I knew it," he said, and stopped dancing. She moved against him to continue the dance.

"So I changed all of the clocks in the house."

"No," he said.

"Yes, here this moment with you is one time and at home it is another."

"You actually took your life into your own hands."

"Literally," Mia said.

"You sure did, Mia."

They danced quietly, and then Mia told Miguel Angel, "Tomorrow I'll change the time back and the world will be the same again."

Mia inhaled deeply and felt so contented and happy, happier than she had ever felt before, and it was as if only the present moment existed and the past, her past, was now forgiven. It was a time she would never forget, a jewel in the life of a woman that she would retrieve as a memory whenever the time needed a good memory. As she took a deep sigh and enjoyed her contentment, she heard Rica's anxious voice calling out her name, "Mia! Mia!" She was running toward her with Estanly.

"What's wrong?"

"It's your father, we heard the hum of his Citroën."

"Where is he?"

"There."

Suddenly, there was her father, all six feet of him, with his white *Chacavera*, and dark pants, looking for her. Everything stood still for one moment. Everyone was silent. No one danced. The elders looked as her father walked towards her, and they shook his hands with words like "*Hola, Jefe,*" and the women stared at him and whispered "*Buenas,* Don Suárez." They all stared at her and then at him as if they were at a tennis match. Miguel Angel gained his composure, and like a man, he gave her father his hand in greeting, "*Buenas*, Don Suarez," Miguel Angel said and her father greeted him too.

"Can I dance with my daughter?"

Her hands were shaking and her body was trembling, and her father whispered, "*Cálmate*, people are going to think that you are afraid of me."

Miguel Angel ordered Estanly to put on the Lucho Gatica song, the one about the clock and time, and he winked at Mia. Mia stood there ready to dance with her father. She looked down not daring to look at his face. She remembered the past when as a child she danced on top of his shiny shoes, back then when she felt love and not fear of him.

The music started again, the same song. She could see everyone looking at them. Hearts began to beat again, and people began to talk again, and fathers began to dance with their daughters, too. Mia looked over at Miguel Angel, who smiled at her, and the song began again.

"What am I going to do with you, Mia?" He said. She remained silent.

"I'm losing all of my hair because of you, you know," and she didn't dare look at him. They remained in silence a while, and the air was beginning to fill with the aroma of frankincense.

"I'm sorry for being difficult. I deserve it," he said, and she relaxed in his arms like when she was a child, and they danced together to the Sunday *boleros* blasting from the radio station. He continued, "I wanted to tell you that I love you and that you should go to *La Misa del Gallo* with your friends, but when I looked at the time and then I looked at my watch, they were different times. I wondered if a little egg that is the young woman I love changed the clocks in the house."

She laughed.

"You forgot to change my watch, Mia," he said and he showed her.

"Oh,"

"Next time," he said, "But today we'll all go to *la Misa del Gallo*," and when she looked over to the corner, she saw Julia with her mother. "She was feeling better," he said, "and I thought she needed some fresh air and conversation."

Mia began to cry.

"Hey, it's ok. I do hope those are tears of joy."

"*Sí, sí,*" she said, "They are." Then they danced and her father began to sing, "*Ella es la estrella que alumbra mi ser yo sin su amor no soy nada.*" He told her that she was indeed his star that illuminated his soul and that without her he was nothing.

Wildflow

It was a warm Sunday morning, and Tati stirred in her pink lounge chair and massaged her sweaty neck. She dried her chest with her damp *panuelo* by placing it gently on her chest and leaving it close to her heart. It was beating fast today. She noticed her books were next to Julio's sunglasses, which were to close to the edge of the table, and so she moved them away, placing them closer to Zuleika. They were having a Sunday brunch at el Embajador hotel and Tati was growing inpatient with her daughter's increasing defiance.

Zuleika stared at her mother and took the black sunglasses with mirrored shades and started playing with them, opening and closing their stems while her mother spoke.

Tati placed her *Aprenda Inglés en una Semana* book on her lap, but it was making her sweat in between her thighs so she put the book on the lounge table, slamming it a bit to make her point with Zuleika.

"I just can't believe what you did," her mother said about the fact that Zuleika, was wearing a tampon under her suit and had the nerve to want to swim in the pool. Now, as a punishment, her mother refused to let her in the water with her cousin Mia, her friend Rica and the boy she liked, Mariano.

Zuleika was happy when her mother finally fell silent. From afar she could see a large rain cloud approaching like the belly of a whale. Suddenly the clouds swept quickly over the sky, allowing the sun to peek through. The sunglasses were strange, mirrored ones, and she stared at her distorted image and smiled. She put them on. She liked the colors of the world through these glasses. The women looked tall and dark pink, and their bodies oily and seductively appealing. Slowly her sadness transformed to awe and excitement about life. The world was so beautiful, and the people were so pretty too. She wanted to touch the women. She took the sunglasses off and looked at them, and she saw her image in them reflected in the glass.

What an ingenious idea, she thought, to hide oneself with sunglasses that made others see their own reflection. It felt safe to see the world like this. Eyes were like windows— people could see your sadness, your happiness, and your insecurities by looking at them. Eyes never lied. Eyes told stories, truths. No wonder movie stars wore glasses like these—it was the only way to keep a little bit of themselves hidden from the public.

Zuleika could see Mia, Mariano and Rica in the pool. For a moment they seemed liked three girls, Mariano blended so nicely with them. Zuleika liked that about him, the girl-like qualities he possessed, the fact that he was so beautiful like a doll. When she wanted to tease him, she'd say, "I will be your girl. I will be your boy," and he would run after her, pin her to the floor, and threaten to kiss her. He never did, though she wished he would. Zuleika was not allowed to see boys or be with them, but Mariano was like family, and his thin, androgynous appearance and his good manners made the elders trust him. So, they bent the rules when it came to Mariano, who often hung out with the girls as if he was one of them.

Whereas her parents protected Rica and Zuleika from boys, they allowed them full freedom to sleep with girls. It was with Rica that she satisfied her basic sexual curiosity. Rica had been her foundation for future loving and future pleasures. She thought of the soothing times she spent with her when they visited the family's summerhouse in Villa Cacata. Other times, Rica would come and sleep over, and they would bathe at night, touching each other in the shower, and at night they would satisfy every longing. It was lovely, Zuleika thought, the feelings they had for each other. It felt good, and what was good could only be holy.

Zuleika touched the sunglasses. She took a deep breath, and she felt confident watching the world through eyes that couldn't see her, and therefore not judge her. She hated the looks of adults, their constant judgment. She loved everything so intensely—the soothing sound of the ocean, the mild breeze that caressed her face, the feel of the rain on her body, the scent of men and women. Was she crazy?

Tati stared at Zuleika and took a deep breath. She noticed that Zuleika was looking at Rica. She was proud of Zuleika's friendship with Rica. Despite her problems in the Bronx, Rica was a good person, always respectful and caring of her elders. Was it her fault that she had fallen in love with an older man who should have know better than to take away her innocence? He was the adult, completely in control, he should have known better. He should have stopped it as soon as it started. It was a good idea to send her to her maternal aunt in Santo Domingo, here life was simpler and men more respectable. The Bronx was not the place to raise young girls.

Tati glanced towards the pool, which was crowded with the tall, voluptuous bodies of women clad with bikinis and five-inch high heels. Why did they wear those high heels to the pool? she wondered. She could hear the women talk about Julio, *"Mira ese es un Papi Chulo,"* one woman said as she looked at him in the bar. Tati was appalled. Tati's heart took a leap and she took a deep breath as if breathing would calm it. She stared at the women's legs, tanned, strong, and felt disturbed and aroused by their presence. She took her compact out of her beach bag and powdered her oily face. She looked pretty at forty-five years old, she thought, and there was strength in her soul that she had lacked when she was younger.

She looked at the women again, their strong legs, tight bodies, and erect breasts. Their composure was mildly erotic and exciting to her. They were so confident about their looks, about what their bodies aroused in others, and they walked around without shame. Tati looked at her legs. They were strong and had many more years to go. She looked down

towards her sweaty breasts, Well, she thought, they may not
be as strong and erect, but they kept their promise.

As Tati thought of this, she took a deep sigh and stared at
her daughter Zuleika, who was wearing Julio's mirrored
sunglasses.

"Look, Mami, you can see your reflection on the mirror
of these glasses," Zuleika said as she faced her mother.
Suddenly, Tati felt her heart stir as she saw her distorted
image in the mirrored sunglasses, and she squinted to see
herself in these sunglasses that belonged to her lover Julio.
Tati looked at herself in them, and she saw a distorted, wide,
old shiny version of herself, and she didn't like it. What would
Julio say if she looked like that? she wondered.

"Take them off, Zuleika."

"*Pero*, Mami, Why?"

"Just take them off."

"*Pero* Mami, look you can see yourself, too, Mami,"
Zuki said as she came closer.

"Take them off now," Tati said and suddenly remembered
when she was younger and first went into the fun house at
Palisades.

Tati remembered her laughter, her joy of living, how she
was with her late husband, who loved her so much. Now, all
she had was Zuleika, and she was strangling her, blocking
her from becoming the woman she could be. Why was it like
that? Why couldn't it be different? Why couldn't she allow
Zuleika to be who she was? She was a strong girl who wanted
to be free from the confines placed on her as a woman. A girl
who could grow wherever she went. Nothing would stop her.
She smiled as she thought that there was this wild part of her
in Zuleika, the part that she never allowed herself to express
as a child, the part of herself that she had hidden after her
husband's death, the part that was beginning to surface now
that she met Julio.

"You are like a wildflower," Tati said to Zuleika in
Spanish, "*Una flor salvaje.*"

"Like a what?" Zuki asked.

"*Una flor silvestre, de estas de campo,*" A wildflower, a wild flower like the ones that grow wild in the hills, and even on the street in concrete; they just grow all over the place just like that; that is what you are—a disobedient wild flower," Tati said.

Zuleika took off the glasses and stared at her mother. "That's not a nice thing to say to a person, Má."

A wildflower, she thought, and a red fire burned in her chest. A wild little flower. A wild thing that grew out of nothing, in concrete, cement, and gave birth to itself on a hill, or in the mountains, that made her really mad.

There was a silence between them, and Tati broke it trying to make amends, "It's not so bad to be a wildflower, Zuki. I'm just saying you're strong. You'll grow anywhere, overcome anything, fight back, not accept what you don't consider right, and I like that, really I do."

Zuleika glanced towards her mother with a smile. She really was a strong person, strong and wild and resilient like those wild flowers that grew on concrete on highways and in mountains, free to be who they were, just free to be. Yes, she would grow no matter what. She liked that. She moved towards her mother and touched her hand, and her mother held it tightly in hers.

"I'm sorry, Zuki, it's just that everything is happening so fast, and I worry more about you now than when you were six."

Zuleika laughed because she remembered the freedom her mother gave her when she was six versus the constraints of her adolescent life. She took off the sunglasses and gave them to her mother as Julio approached and handed Zuleika her *refresco rojo* and her mother the Piña Colada she ordered.

"*Gracias*, Julio," Tati said, and Julio sat down next to her.

Tati took a deep sigh and sipped from her Piña Colada, while she and Zuleika exchanged silent glances that augured a period of change for both of them. Zuleika needed experiences, she needed to learn. Zuleika smiled and looked toward the distant sky. The large gray cloud seemed to have increased in size but did not move towards them. Mia waved for her to come into the pool, and Rica was beginning to come out of the water to get her. Rica was dripping wetness from her well-developed body. Her breasts were huge and hard and did not bounce. Her nipples were hard and exposed through the wet bathing suit. She walked cautiously towards Zuleika.

"*Buenas tardes*," Rica said.

"*Buenas*, Rica, and how is your aunt?" Tati asked.

"Much better, thank you."

"Who are you with?" Tati asked.

"My cousins and Estanly," she said and pointed to the young Dominican girls with their tall, tanned voluptuous bodies in high heels and the young man they were catering to, a twenty-two year old disk jockey from the local radio station.

Tati had heard of him. Politically, he was Rica's uncle by adoption, she thought. She stared at him and she recalled not liking how he looked at Rica, as if he owned her. Now, in the pool with Mia, she noticed how he seductively stared at her as if he wanted her.

Uncomfortable by Tati's growing suspicions, Rica said to Zuleika, "Come on sweetie, it's time to go in, the water. You're going to boil out here."

Zuleika glanced towards her mother and then at Julio, "Go, go on. Go, it'll be fun," he said, and Tati silently agreed.

"Well, what the hell are you waiting for? Go ahead and have a time," her mother said in English, but left out the "good."

Zuleika got up from her sticky chair, took off her shorts, and walked quickly away from her mother after whispering a "thanks," and Rica hugged her and whispered, "Mariano is dying to talk to you. You have to watch Mia—she wants everybody." And they watched as Mia spoke to Mariano in a way that seemed loving and sweet. Zuleika's heart filled with joy at the anticipation of being with him, and her footsteps quickened, but suddenly she heard the thunderous sound of her mother's voice.

"Zuleika" her mother screamed. She looked back.

"Don't run. You could fall, The flower is slippery," her mother said in her accented English.

"The flower?" they asked together as they looked back at her mother. She was always pronouncing everything wrong, "Kiss, for keys" and "Bitch for beach," and "Shit, for sheets," but "flower for floor" This was a new one that sent them into a fits of laughter.

"I mean the floor is slippery," her mother said.

Rica and Zuleika continued laughing as they walked towards the pool. Their laughter echoed in the distance.

"Is your flower slippery?" Rica asked, and Zuleika responded with a "Do you want to find out?" and they laughed some more as they walked towards Mariano, who suddenly looked like a man to Zuleika and no longer the adolescent boy. He was sitting at the edge of the pool dripping wet and waiting.

Amor es... Love is

Julia, our housekeeper, has prepared breakfast. A cafe con leche, six *pan de aguas con mantequilla,* our daily bread. A *pan de agua* is a small Dominican baguette the size of the palm of my hand. Its shape reminds me of a miniature woman's private part. It's the way the Dominican *panaderos* fold the bread with such tenderness, oval shaped with a slit in the middle. I suppose to make them look like they have two labias just like a vagina. Before I eat, I pray, *un padre nuestro.*

Julia thinks I am too skinny by Dominican standards, and so she brings three more of those little breads and fills my cup with warm coffee. I touch the bread, and it is warm and soft like love when it is new and forbidden. I take one and open it right in the middle, and I can see a little steam come out, forming in the air like a genie. I praise God and bless the vagina bread I am given every morning when others have very little. I take a knife and spread Dominican butter right in the middle, and I watch how the butter melts and penetrates all of the crevices of the warm bread, and then I bite into it very slowly and oh it has a crunchy feel, and softness unfolds inside of my mouth like longing.

My father is eating breakfast and calmly reading his *Listín Diario,* his daily bread. He reads that newspaper every day. He's draped with it like an umbrella so that you can't see him. My mother is arguing with me over whom I can and can't hang out with. She doesn't like some of my friends. "I know what's up with Rica and Estanly," Mami says. Rica is my best friend from the Bronx. She's like a sister to me. Rica lives with her aunt here in Santo Domingo because her parents are afraid she'll get pregnant in the Bronx. What they don't know is that she does whatever she wants in Santo Domingo because her aunt is always depressed, and her grandparents who live three blocks away dote on her.

Rica's grandparents live with their adopted youngest son, twenty-two-year old Estanly. Technically this makes him Rica's uncle, but not really because they just met this year and they are not blood relatives. Rica says he's the man of her dreams, her soul mate. Estanly is cool. He's *el Disjoki*, the local DJ, for a radio station that brings the greatest American music to the island if it isn't censored by the president. Estanly has long, light brown hair that waves in the humid hot air and light-colored eyes. He reminds me of this boy I once knew named Snake.

My mother continues asking me about Rica and Estanly. She feels Rica is a bad influence and that people will think badly of me for hanging out with her. My mother worries a lot about "*él que dirán,*" what others say. She feels people are very judgmental here in Santo Domingo. It's all about appearances.

"Tell me the truth."

"What truth?" I ask her.

"Is she dating Estanly?"

"Why?"

My father butts in from behind the *Listín*. "Why? Don't be disrespectful asking your mother why. Answer her."

My mother looks at me, proud that he's come to her defense against my adolescent rebellion.

"No," I lie.

"Then he better not be interested in you," Papi says from behind his curtain of words.

"It's not right, Ynoemia," Mami says. "*Ése se le ve cara de vampiro,*"

"*Un vampiro*, Mami?"

"Mia!" Papi says in a tone that says "watch your tone."

Mami goes on and on about how you open a door to a vampire like him, and the next thing you know, he wants to be in your bed. Bed. Sex has not even been on my mind when it comes to Estanly, but now that they put it there like a seed, it begins to grow.

Mami finds Estanly too old to be hanging out with us *niñas*, but here in this country, older boys and men like very young girls. They like them young and tender, like clay you can mold.

Estanly reminds my mother of her past, of men she once knew so she is always afraid for me. Papi goes back to reading his *Listín Diario* very peacefully and she turns to him for support. He undrapes himself and sets the *Listín* on the table. He stares at the Mont Blanc pen he's bought me and my journal that says *"Gobierno Dominicano"* where he told me to document my history. They are right next to me, bothering no one but him. It's my daily bread to write after breakfast and before I go to bed. Now, he gives me one of his ultimatums.

"The next time I see you speaking to Estanly, I'll take your pen."

The thought of his taking my pen away makes my heart freeze for a moment. I stare at him in disbelief, and he looks very pleased.

School here is not like the Bronx. They expect a lot from their students, and high school is like college. I attend *El Colegio Santo Domingo*, a private, all-girl, Catholic high school. I am in the English program. Most of the wealthy Dominican girls are all very light-skinned. They look like American girls. Some of them are snotty. They do not like us Dominican girls who were raised in New York, particularly the Bronx, so I don't hang out with them. Mostly, they try to be decent, but behind our backs they think we are low class. They call us names like *"Gringas Sucia"* but not to our faces. The rich girls, they hang out with each other. The Bronx girls, they hang out with each other. We are not invited to the parties of the rich girls. It's strange to wait so long to come to your own country and then feel like you don't belong.

Most of my family works for the government. Papi says these are dangerous times, everywhere. Papi is worried because there is constant criticism of the government and the President. He fears that the Dominican Republic will become another Cuba. Just recently, the country was again in turmoil, Francisco Alberto Caamano, the leader of the 1965 revolution that the United States troops were sent to put down, was shot and killed while leading a guerrilla movement against Joaquin Balaguer. I tried to cut it out of the newspaper to create a collage of stories about this time, but Papi didn't let me. He took away the scissors and the paper and said, "This can get you into a lot of trouble, Mia. I know he felt bad for censoring me because the following week he bought me one of the *cuadernos* from the Palace where the men document our history, he said, "Here Mia, use this to document your history." I felt it was the nicest thing he's ever done.

So, I am not allowed to go anywhere unescorted and Papi supervises my every move. He did let me go to la Jamona's house, Doña Beatriz, who lives three houses away at the corner, near Rocky Bear's where most of the young people hang out. She's this cool old woman, *bien Chevere,* like they say here. She loves teenagers, and we have all become her children. She treats us like we matter and have brains, and I respect that. She tells us to love our country above all and freedom along with it. She speaks and we listen to her. She tells us stories about the past when you couldn't say a word in this country without dying. She says nothing has changed. Her husband disappeared during the dictatorship while she was waiting at the altar. She heard that the secret police came and took him late at night. She never married. In front of her house she has a *muro*, a bench, dedicated to him. Papi is suspicious of her and wonders if she's a communist. Papi is afraid of communism. He wouldn't let me hang out there last night, but after much begging and the support from Zuki's mom, Tati, he let me go. Tati said these were our best years, and we couldn't be cooped up in a house. As soon as he consented, I ran out for fear that he may change his mind like he did for Valentine's Day. Once there, I had a great time. I was with my cousin Zuki and the guys Estanly, Chici, Mavi, Panchi and Polanco.

Estanly, Rica's boyfriend, treated me to two bingo games because I was broke, *pela* as they say here. Rica was sick with a cold and so he treated me as if I was his girl. When he looked at me with his light eyes I saw myself in them, and then I stopped because I'm in love with this sixteen year old, Miguel Angel, this beautiful Dominican boy who lives on Calle Libra, and who reminds me of David Cassidy, but after a wonderful Christmas celebration he stopped speaking to me. I think it has something to do with my father, and the fact that his father is a member of the Dominican Revolutionary Party. Sometimes, I wonder if he misses me. So now that Estanly is showing interest in me and looking at me like I'm the only person who matters to him, I find my thoughts straying. For a moment, I thought I belonged to Estanly, to this tall young man with the voice of an angel.

After Bingo, Estanly walked me home. He wanted me to know that he found out that Miguel Angel was just playing with me. "*Sólo estaba jugando contigo*," he said and stated that I was too good and didn't deserve that. I froze for a moment, but didn't let him know how much it hurt me. "Playing with me"—even now, the words are ringing in my ear. Then, Estanly said to forgive him because he knew it was wrong, but he needed to confess, and he blurted out, "One falls in love and there is nothing one can do," and I said, "Es, *por favor*," and he said he loved it when I call him Es and that from that moment on, he would no longer be Estanly, but "Es," and I laughed, and he went on, "The truth is I've loved you since the first time I saw you, and I can feel your love for me too," and he pointed out that when we looked at each other during Bingo, he could feel how strongly we connected, "*Había algo especial entre nosotros*," he said, that there was this special something between us. We felt for each other. I liked the sound of his voice when he said that. I felt like a woman for a moment and not a child, but then I realized that he thinks I'm easy prey, and as we were walking I heard the hum of my father's Citroén coming towards us, and we stood there, just stood there, and Papi stopped and said, "Get in the car, Ynoemia," and that was it. At night, Estanly dedicates songs to me, the Stylistics, Roberta Flack or Barry White. They remind me of the Bronx.

So, Papi caught me talking to Es, and I couldn't write for a week. He took my pen and I couldn't sit on the porch until I learned my lesson. I told him that Es is a friend. He's close to my other friends, but Papi wouldn't hear it. I promised I'd be careful because I don't want to be locked up in here and not be allowed the simple pleasure of writing, visiting Mona on Bingo night, walking to Rica's or to Rocky Bear's where we buy *refresco rojo*.

Today, I was in Rica's house watching Cleopatra, and Es came and now they're back in love again. I started to feel really angry, but couldn't understand my reaction. Her aunt, who is always sad and sleeping, was in bed so we had the house for ourselves. Es started to kiss Rica to the point that I could see his tongue in her mouth and when I saw his tongue entering her mouth, he would open his eyes and look at me. He has these beautiful eyes and lips. I watched, and for a moment I wondered how it would be to have his tongue in my mouth. I wanted him in that second and wished that Rica would let me kiss him like when we were in the Bronx and we would play spin the bottle and watch each other kiss each other, Pito, Snake, Eva, Rica and Zuki and I. We wouldn't get jealous of each other. It didn't matter back then, but now that we are growing up, all of that seemed like child's play.

I went out on the porch so they could be by themselves in the living room because I wasn't going to *aguantar gorro,* as they say here. Rica went to the bathroom, and he came out on the porch and said, "You look sad," and "What's wrong, *querida?*" and I wanted to cry.

He tried to touch me, and I asked him to keep his hands off me, and then he brushed my cheek with his lips, lingering close to my mouth. He didn't really kiss me, though, but he left me filled with desire, my heart sinking down to my *pompo* private part.

"You want me, right, Mia?" he whispered, and I realized what power the sound of his sweet voice had upon me, for I had goose bumps all over.

I stood there with all these feelings I hadn't had since Pito, and then he said, "I want you to tell yourself the truth. Look in your heart and say to yourself how much you feel for me, as much as I feel for you, and tonight I want you to be honest, just be honest, and write me a letter expressing these feelings. Tell me the truth and call me at midnight."

I wrote him a letter, but I didn't see him at midnight.

It's been days since I've seen Es and Rica. In the afternoon, I find excuses to go over to his house. I thought Rica might be there with him, but they weren't there. My cousin Zuki came to visit, and I went to the bedroom to show her all of the things Mami brought me from her short trip to New York. My cousin Eva sent me some halter tops, which Papi is refusing to let me wear because my back will be exposed. I can't wear any blouse that exposes my belly button. My father thinks a belly button is a private part.

I'm showing Zuki all of my goodies when the bell rings and it's Estanly. "*Hola,*" he said, standing there knowing that if Papi sees me speaking to him I won't be able to write. Zuki couldn't stop giggling, and when she giggles she sounds like she's crying.

Papi called out from the bedroom where he was taking care of my ailing mother, "Why is Zuki crying?" and as I went into the house, I said, "Crying?"

I guess my question raised his suspicions because he said, "Who's at the door this time?"

"At the door?"

"Yes, at the door. I heard the doorbell ring,"

"No one."

Then he looked at me and I could tell he knew I was lying.

"Is it Estanly?" he said and made a gesture to smack my face, and then he just grabbed me by my chin and said, "The next time I see you with him, I will break your face," but I know he won't.

I stood there, in front of my father, my body shaking. I know that Es is not good for me, but it's like I'm drawn to the fire and the more Papi doesn't want me with him, the more attractive he becomes. I've been sneaking around and kissing with Es when I know I shouldn't, but I do. We live by secret gestures of love, glances, words with double meaning, secret evening phone calls, and kisses we long to give each other, but can't.

Papi continues screaming, that I thought he was a *pendejo*, that Es is no good and can ruin my life and my reputation. "Can't you see what he's doing?" he asked, "Men like him only want one thing, Ynoemia, one thing! Do you want me to go out on the porch and kick his ass?" I asked him not to do that.

I went out on the porch, very embarrassed, my cheeks red, my eyes teary, and my chin bruised, and Zuki was with Es, and I said to him, "Strange to see you around here."

"What's his problem?" he asked.

I acted as if nothing had happened. Es looked at me and said I'd left him standing on the porch for five minutes and where was my respect. I apologized and then he questioned me about Papi, and I told him that there was no problem and then he said that he heard it all, and I said that I was so sorry that he had, but that my father thinks I'm dating him. He started to laugh, "He thinks we are in love?" and I said, "Yes, he does think that," and he smiled and then he asked me, "What do you think?"

I said I didn't know, and then he said to Zuki, "We're in love you know," and he held my hand and Zuki stopped laughing and looked at me. I said it wasn't true, and then I felt it was, and I said it was, and then I said it wasn't, and she asked me "What about Miguel Angel?" and I said "We haven't spoken for months," and I couldn't stop looking at Estanly, and he said "I'm not on speaking terms with Miguel Angel, either," and he added "So I don't want to hear that you are speaking to him," and I laughed, but Zuki didn't. I thought it was a joke, but I couldn't understand really. Then Zuki and I stood there in silence, staring at him and wondering what to say and what to do and then Zuki looked at him and she looked at me, and she walked away without saying goodbye.

Rica and I go to the same school, and we are in the same class, but we no longer speak to each other. Es asked me not to try to speak to her at all, that she isn't a good friend to me. Rica wrote me a note saying, "I have missed you," and we made up. She confessed that Es is the love of her life, and they will get married when she's eighteen, and all that bullshit he's been telling me. Later when I passed Rica's to go to Rocky Bear's I saw them in the living room and he was holding her. I left. Today, Rica is celebrating their five month anniversary. She acts like she's been dating him for five years. When she left, he came close to me and said, "Come to my house during siesta when my parents are asleep."

My heart was beating fast, and I was sweating with joy at hearing his voice. It is so sweet and mellow, like Barry White singing in Spanish. When I arrived, his parents were sleeping. He grabbed me when I entered and kissed me with such hunger—his lips sucking my lips, my neck, and shoulders, his hands caressing me all over as if I were going to disappear. I couldn't breathe; all I could think of was that

107

no one has loved me like this before. Es said that he couldn't stop thinking about me, something about my pants, the shorts I had on, my halter top exposing my back, my breasts, how they show through my thin blouse.

Then he said that when a woman loves someone, nothing she does is wrong and not to worry. I got scared. We stood there in silence and then as I moved away to leave, he grabbed me by the wrist and he said, "Mia," and he stopped and thought carefully about what he was going to say.

"I thought I asked you not to sit on the porch."

"Yes,"

"Do you write?"

"Yes, I sit and write,"

"What did I ask you?"

"You asked me not to do it."

"Then why are you doing it?

"Because a woman should write her own history. Papi said that to me the day he gave me my pen and my *Gobierno Dominicano* notebook. "

"But, didn't I ask you not to do that?"

"Yes, but I want to document my history,"

"No, Mia, that's what men are here to do."

I stood still for a moment wondering what to say and not being able to say anything because it was as if he had cut off my hands.

"Do you want me to stop breathing too?"

He grabbed me by the wrist real hard and pushed me towards him.

"Don't you ever talk to me like that, Mia," and he added that I was disrespectful. When he saw I was almost going to cry, he apologized, "Mia, mi amor," and he kissed my wrist, "Look what you made me do to you," he said as he looked at the bruise that formed on my thin wrist.

"Am I important to you?" and I didn't answer, so he asked again, and I found myself lying so that I could leave and never see him again. I knew then that my parents were right about him. He was a vampire, draining women from their source, their power. What recipe would my Aura use to keep him at bay—a string of garlic, with thyme and sprinkled with vinegar and rose water? Yes.

I knew, too, that I couldn't be with a man who did not want me to write. Never. Writing was my daily bread, and I would not give it up for anyone. So when he asked me, "Do you love me?" I said "Sure," and he looked at me because he sensed something different in me.

"I have to go now," I said, "or my father will find out that I'm not in my bedroom during siesta."

As I walked away from him, I was crying over what I've done to Rica and myself and crying for what he'd done to Rica. Then that afternoon, after siesta, I sat on the porch with my notebook and my pen. My daily bread.

For weeks I did not speak to Estanly. When he called, I hung up. I no longer needed the drama of his love. I didn't like what I was doing to Rica, who had been such a good friend to me for so long. I promised myself that I would never again be with a man who has another woman. At night, his radio station was blasting sad American songs, but I didn't call him or answer his desperate calls. When in desperation he dared to come over to my house, I told Julia to tell him off and send him away, "*Pero, Señorita,*" Julia would say, "*Ese es el Señorito* Estanly," as if he were someone important.

Then one day as I was walking towards Rocky Bear's for a *refresco rojo*, there was Miguel Angel, this boy I used to love. He was there standing in front of Rocky Bear's. He wiped his lips with the back of his right hand .

"*Hola,*" he said, and I couldn't respond.

For a moment, my whole life stood suspended in time. I couldn't speak. His brother, Rafi, gave me his hand, "*Hola!*" he said, and I said "*Hola,*" but looked at Miguel Angel.

"*Hola*," Miguel Angel said and gave me his hand. Suddenly, I felt a thousand feelings in his "*Hola.*"

That night we spoke on the phone and we were like old friends again. Then he said, "*Mia, perdóname,*" and explained his neglect. I told him I was upset for some time. He said he never meant to hurt me with his silence. He asked if we could start again, if he could call me and I said yes. The whole night, I replayed his *Hola* and the image of his hand touching my hand, the whole night I thought of him.

Time flies. I have not spoke to Estanly for a very long time. He's history. I've moved on with my life. It is April. Semana Santa is a strange festive family event. So, on Saturday Papi said I couldn't write because it was Holy Week. I was furious. I had to go to bed early, too, because Papi said we should honor the holy season. We are in my aunt's summer house, but I'm dying to get home so that I can talk to Miguel Angel.

On Saturday, with Papi's permission, I went to a party two houses from ours. Zuki, Polanco and Miguel Angel were there. Miguel Angel and I sat there and looked at the evening sky. We talked about his involvement in the youth movement supporting the liberation of the Dominican Republic, that's what he calls it. If Papi heard me talking about liberation, for sure I'd be sent back to the Bronx. I didn't understand a lot of what he was saying, but he was trying to teach me things about our country. I wish my father and I could talk about these things. I see other fathers, how they talk to their daughters—they don't want them to be ignorant about world's affairs. A woman needs to be rounded, full of knowledge.

So, Miguel Angel, goes on and tells me that the social democratic movement aims to remove all of the injustices we were seeing in our country. He told me to open my eyes and see, to see the poverty, the inequality and then to do everything in my power to change it. "Learn the history of your country," he said, and he added "For in our history is our destiny."

Miguel Angel went on to proudly say that one day he would be part of that liberation and that he was going to *La Universidad* to study in order to become part of the change. Suddenly, I too wanted to be part of his life and part of that change.

I don't know what's wrong with me—all I think is about Miguel Angel, the way he talks to me about change and liberation. I read the history of our country to figure out how I can help in shaping its destiny. At night, I wish I was with Miguel Angel, that we could lie down on the wet grass and look up at the sky while he tells me stories about the rose and the cross, about the Rosicrucians. I daydream about the way he loves me and kisses me. I'm surprised because it was just recently that I felt this way for Es. Could this be love or just infatuation? When he calls me we talk about life. Last night, we spoke for a long time, about school, his upcoming graduation. I spoke about my charity work at the orphanage, and going back to teaching the trabajadoras how to read and write. He says he's proud of me. He feels that the most noble person has a focus on community and the improvement of one's country. My chest was burning with pride.

Today, Má and Pá *se la lucieron* in front of everyone. Papi smacked me with a book by Karl Marx, some manifesto I had borrowed from Miguel Angel, and he said "That's the kind of shit that can get you killed." He was so angry.

"Who gave you this?" he asked.

"I borrowed it from Tío's library," I lied, but I knew he wouldn't believe me. My uncle had an extensive collection of socialist books next to the one's on UFO's, which such titles as *Mysterious Visitors* or *Alien from Space,"*and *They Are Not From Here.*

If I told him the truth, he would never let me talk to

Miguel Angel. Then Papi ordered me to return the book to my uncle before it was too late, but I sensed he knew it belonged to someone else.

Lately, Papi has been angry at my behavior. I sneak out of the house when he's not here, and he wants me to stay with Mami who is sick. I'm afraid of staying with my mother because she's lost thirty pounds and it frightens me. I feel guilty for not wanting to be her nurse. I think her illness has something to do with the cancer she once had in her breast, but no one talks about it. It's a secret. To monitor my late night phone calls, Papi has developed a system where if I dial my phone from my bedroom, he can hear it because the phone rings in his. How he did it, I don't know. I've developed my own system to outdo his. If I dial the phone upside down, it doesn't ring in his bedroom.

Today, I was very confused and sad. I went to Rocky Bear's for candy and I saw Miguel Angel and Zuki there. I had tears in my eyes. They asked what was wrong with me, and they came and both hugged me real tight when I told them I thought my mother was dying. I started to cry and they both hugged me and kissed me. "We are here for you," they said and Zuki kissed me on one cheek and Miguel Angel on the other, and they showered me with kisses on my nose and eyes and they made me laugh.

Today, my mother was kind to me, apologizing for the times she had not been a good mother, and I could see in the shifting of her eyes and the movement of her body that she was hiding something from me, and my heart skipped a beat, and I knew that her trip to New York had to do with the secrets she keeps from me. "You are such a good person, Mia," she said, "and I'll remember that forever. This was truly a mother and daughter's day."

I was lying on my bed while we spoke, and the night was warm with the scent of roses coming from our neighbor's garden. Miguel Angel explained about the Rosicrucians, and the symbols of the Rose and the Cross.

"The rose and the cross were symbols dating back to the thirteenth century," he said and added, "They represent divine wisdom through love and knowledge. It's this idea of loving all living things."

"I like this idea of divine wisdom and love. Love is faith. Love is wisdom."

"The world is full of mysteries, Mia, and the old one's knew so much more than we did. They believed that within us was the truth, if we just sat and listen to it, but we are so distracted by greed, and need."

I thought of the spirit world, how back when I was thirteen I could communicate with the dead through the Ouija Board, my talking board. I told him about my cousin Aura and how we cleansed and healed *el Doctor* from his sexual desires for children and how we could cure the sick with a *paso de mano* and a prayer.

And suddenly, the world was clear and simple. The feeling of love and safety. I felt so secure in my love for him, the kind of security that makes you feel like you flow with life, the stars, the moon, like there is this rhythm, this expectation, this comfort, this structure in your life, and he's that for me, and so I felt so close to him.

After a great week with Miguel Angel, the world has taken an unexpected spin and my life is in chaos. As we were walking *el barrio*, Polanco, Zuki, Miguel Angel and I, they began to speak poorly of Estanly.

"Estanly es un hombre abusivo," Polanco said and pointed out how some men know that they are seducing young women and don't care of the consequences. They pointed out that Estanly has been with Yadira, Chichi's sister who has just turned thirteen. They also mentioned that

Estanly has tried to mess around with Mavi's twelve year old sister and Mavi kicked Estanly's ass.

Then Miguel Angel said he could never date a girl who has dated Estanly.

Polanco went on to say that he can never blame a young woman, but Miguel Angel said, *"Son mis valores."*

"It's not their fault. A girl of twelve is still a child. What does she know," Polanco added.

Zuki and I walked together in silence, not saying much. My heart was suddenly in the sweaty palm of my hand while I walked with him. There was a blackout. The air was hot and humid. I couldn't breathe.

What if Estanly told Miguel Angel about us? Would he leave me?

"¿Estás bien?" Miguel angel asked.

"Sí," I said and suddenly his lips were on mine warm and hard. As we were kissing we could hear Polanco greeting some friends, Chichi, Mavi, Alejandro and Estanly. As our eyesight adjusted to the dark we could tell Estanly had seen the end of our long kiss. The others were laughing about one thing or another. Miguel Angel was behind me, his arms across my chest. In the commotion, Chichi dragged Miguel Angel. "Estanly," Miguel Angel said, *"Dedicamele..."* and he went on to ask Estanly to dedicate a song by the stylistics that I liked very much.

"Sí, sí," Estanly said and took the opportunity to come close to me so that I could tell him the song, but instead he whispered, *"Que estupido yo e sido. Que maldita hipocrita tú eres."*

After Estanly saw me with Miguel Angel, he's been calling me to insult me, so I don't pick up the phone. He leaves letters which I do not open, flowers and cards he buys at the local stationery. Last week, I heard that he broke up with Rica and she went crazy. I do not tune into his radio station because it's become so melodramatic with secret messages to me and love songs that must be boring the whole country. Today, Estanly came to the house, apologized to my father, and asked him to tell me. I stayed in my room and when Papi asked me to speak to Estanly, I waved him away.

"What's going on that you don't want to speak to Estanly?"

I said nothing.

"Here," Papi said, and gave me the phone number and the name of a hospital. He explained, Rica had tried to kill herself. I was shocked.

"Do you want me to take you?"

"Yes."

I went to the hospital to see Rica. Her bandaged hands seemed to urge me to come and hug her. I felt guilty, as if I created this chain of events. "I've missed you," she said and reminded me of our bond. I wanted to cry but felt like rock inside. I left reminding myself that my life was valuable, far more valuable than my love for a man. I promised myself that suicide would never be a solution to my life's problems.

I snuck out of the house during siesta time to see Miguel Angel and talk about Rica's suicide attempt. He was angry at Estanly. Miguel Angel seemed joyful to see me, and we kissed for long moments. Luscious kisses that defied our ability to need air, holding each other as if something stonger than ourselves was separating us. Then, his mother caught us. She looked at me with her vicious dagger and made it clear how she felt about me. She escorted him to the kitchen without saying one word. Once there I could hear her angry muffled words. She scolded sharply and asked him if he was out of his mind and then said, *"sacamela de aqui, por favor."* She said the *por favor* slowly, but loud enough so that I could hear it. I felt worthless. She reminded me of Tía Martirio when she scolded me and kicked me out her house. Her words are still in my head, *"vete de aqui muda e mierda."* There are words that slices you up and bad looks that shrink you into a little shrivel of nothingness. I called him twice today, but his mother says that he is not there, although Zuki said he was sitting on the porch.

Miguel Angel doesn't call me as frequently anymore. After several attempts at reaching him, he returned my call and we met at Rocky Bear's. He bought me *Triangulito de Nestlé*, condensed milk inside a small triangular shaped container, and you suck and suck the sweetest milk out of it, and it is like love, so he buys them for me and we stare at each other while I suck on the *Triangulitos*. I have this feeling he wants to tell me something, but he can't. Today he looks at me and he coughs. Then he says, "Do you keep any secrets from me?" he asked.

"Like what?"

"Secrets."

"Well, I think people have stories that they keep to themselves, stuff that happens...but..."

"Those are secrets."

"What would it mean to you, if I kept a secret from you?"

He didn't answer.

I have not heard from Miguel Angel for three weeks and at this point I wondered if we are together. Zuki says not to think that way. I feels he's changed, but he won't say why and when I ask he says it's in my head. Today, I finally spoke to him. He said he was busy. I was excited about seeing him at Panchi's party. I wanted to talk to him about life, love and esoteric things, about why I kept secrets from him.

Papi didn't want to let me go, and Panchi's mother came and gave him a respectful lecture on adolescence and how adolescents needed to see each other and talk and all. Papi told her not to tell him how to raise his daughter, and she apologized. But he let me go, and before I left he said, "That woman better not come asking for you to stay longer."

Miguel Angel came with his cousin Bebe, the Haitian

beauty. She is tall, brown-skinned with long dark hair and large brown eyes, and a strict father, which increased her net worth and value. Most of all, she spoke French, which killed me because French and everything French is of great importance in Santo Domingo. They love the French here. So mostly I was trying to get to know Bebe, who seems like a mature girl for her age.

Miguel Angel was sweet to me despite the fact that we have not spoken much. He asked about school, my mother and he introduced me to Bebe. No one would have known that for the past few weeks he'd been distant. Throughout the night, he was attentive to his cousin, so I didn't bother to question him or ask for explanations.

Estanly asked me to dance and I said no, and when I refused a second time, he dragged me outside by my arm, which was very embarrassing.

"*Coño*," he said, "*Es que tú no tienes verguenza*," telling me I had no shame.

"Let me go," I said.

"Stop acting like a *pendeja*, like you don't know what is going on."

But I didn't know.

"You told him," I said to Estanly, "You told him about us."

He denied it, but I could see he was lying.

I started to walk home alone, and I asked Estanly to leave me alone. At that moment, Miguel Angel ran towards me and said "*Mia, Mi amor, mira perdóname*," he said, and I started to cry.

Miguel Angel and I haven't spoken for three days and when we finally decided to meet *en el muro de la jamona*, it was to talk about us. He wanted to be honest with me, and so he said he was confused because Bebe was in love with him, and she's this incredible girl that his family loves very much, and he's been wondering about us and about her. Then I left with all my sadness like a shadow. He did not speak of Estanly.

I went to the basketball court and some of the guys were there, and Polanco was there, and I said something really stupid.

"Congratulations, I hear you're dating Bebe," and he said "Mia, you know that's not true" as he played with the ball, and then he said "Why don't you tell me the truth?"

"Forget it," I said and walked away.

He ran over to me and hugged me tightly, "*Mi princesa*," he said tenderly, "I'll fix it for you" and promised to talk to Miguel Angel. Then I told him the truth is that Miguel Angel has this pride and he won't let go of it and I said, "he knows, right?"

Polanco lowered his eyes and knew what I was speaking about and he said, "yes."

Polanco told me the truth that Miguel Angel did not want to believe Estanly. They fought and argued about the truth, but Estanly showed him a letter I had written. Miguel Angel was furious.

"He just couldn't deal with it. His pride. You know how he feels about Estanly," Polanco said.

Miguel Angel doesn't pass by my block anymore and the days pass and the nights come, and I don't sit on the porch to write. I feel guilty. I feel like I am the worst person on earth. I wrote him a letter apologizing for my lie of omission and my mistakes with Estanly. He did not call or write back.

Papi wants to know what's wrong, and he brings me notebooks from his job at the Palace, notebooks that say "*Gobierno Dominicano*," hard, huge notebooks that are supposed to be for documenting Dominican history, but Papi brings them to me to document mine. But, I no longer write on the front porch under the stars, listening to the crickets sing. I don't call Miguel Angel because it's no longer my place to do so. I leave Thursday for New York City, but I'll be back.

There is no *Amor es*....
That expresses my sadness and disappointment
Love is sometimes feeling sad
Love is sometimes being disappointed
Love is always changing

When I arrived in New York City, smelling of flowers, ripe mangos and guavas, I found out that Mimi and Rosa are in Puerto Plata visiting family and Eva is in Santiago. Everyone else was all grown up and busy with their lives. The days passed slowly between working at the factory cutting the strings off cheap dresses and taking Mami to see the doctor. I missed my life in Santo Domingo and soon I'll return.

I have just arrived in the country of my heart, and it is still the same. Polanco hugs me, "Mi Princesa," and kisses me and then runs to get Miguel Angel.

"*Hola*," I said. I couldn't believe he had grown so much. I'm about as tall as his chin now, and so I had to stand on tiptoe to kiss him. We walked to *El Paseo de Los Indios*, Zuki and Polanco behind us, engrossed in conversation.

Today I realized that every day I love this country more and more and don't wish to ever leave it. I hope to stay here for the rest of my life—no more packing in a rush to leave in a rush, no more moving to places where no one wants to live, but instead making contacts, establishing relationships, and developing long term friendships. That's what my soul would like.

I love Santo Domingo. I love how everything smells here. You wake up, and you sit on the porch, and the earth is pregnant with scents, the scent of flowers, roses, jasmine, gardenias, hibiscus, the scent of almonds, and the sea-salted scent of the ocean. I fall in love every morning again and again.

I love to walk this *barrio* where I live called *Los Jardines Zodiacales*. I walk to the outskirts of it where there is a *colmado*, Rocky Bear's. I like Rocky Bear's because the boys hang out there, and I get my candy and talk to them. It's always hotter at Rocky Bear's than in other places, and it always smells like chicken shit and almonds.

I love the sound of roosters in the distance, and the *paletero* selling his candy with his little song, "*Paletero, Paletero,*" or the fruit vendor's "*frutas, frutas, frutas, aguacates, aguacates, aguacates.*" All of this is mine to love. I love the smell of rain in the afternoon and how the earth steams up and gives me more gifts, and the sound of the crickets at night singing their song, and the clear view of the stars, and the moon so luminous.

Miguel Angel doesn't call or pass by. I wonder how it is that boys could forget you so easily. One day, they say it's over and it is. Suddenly, you are out of their minds. Women have a different mind. We have a camera placed in our brain that replays all the special moments again and again. It doesn't let us forget. Today after coming back from my aunt's house in La Bolivar, I went straight to Zuki's house. We walked by Miguel Angel's home and he was with Bebe. I wanted the earth to swallow me whole. His older brother was there with his new wife, and she said, "*Ay, Mamá,*" that's like "oh, shit!!" in English.

They all greeted me out of politeness from the porch. I waved back, and Bebe remained silent with a sad smile on her face that told me she did not want to hurt me. I stood there feeling lost in my grief. I walked so fast I left Zuki behind. I couldn't see where I was going because my tears clouded my vision. I told Zuki I wanted to be alone, and I went home.

When I arrived home, Zuki called to say that Miguel

Angel was coming in fifteen minutes to see me. She wanted me to wait for him outside. When he arrived and he held me there in the porch for a long time. His arms holding me so tight and I couldn't speak or cry.

He whispered "I had to come and see you."

I started to cry then and he kissed my tears and said "I just couldn't go to bed wondering how you were feeling."

He wiped my tears with the palm of his hands.

"I don't want to ever hurt you."

Then he kissed my lips, and I didn't care if people saw us.

Suddenly, as we held each other, I felt a profound sense of peace that told me that all would be well. There was this deep acceptance of the ending of our love.

Polanco came by to chat, and Papi greeted him nicely, "*Siéntense en el Patio.*" I was stunned. When we were alone, Polanco said, "*Princesa*, we've had good times, you know."

He said it as if we were going to war, as if our lives were unraveling and coming to an end. He sounded older, or maybe we are all growing up now. He had that wise old man look in his eyes. He went on to remember the old days, Los Aguinaldos during the Christmas of '72, dancing Merengue in the street, Lucho Gatica, "*Reloj no Marques Las Horas,*" and *la Misa del Gallo*, the midnight mass on Christmas Eve, the I Ching, the broom with salt on the New Year, burning it and all to bring in the good spirits of '73, and my passion for reading, giving out books to people, sharing with them, and my writing and reading classes at *las trabajadores* of the Jardines. We laughed as we remember how the President censored a few American songs, particularly Sylvia Robinson's, "Pillow Talk."

"*Un momento, un poquito,*" Polanco said. "And that was enough to get Estanly in trouble, the country in an uproar and the President to assert his authority."

We laughed until our ribs hurt and then there was silence between us.

For a moment, I sensed something new between Polanco and me. A new feel in our friendship. His hands came close to mine and he held them and he said, "It's good to be alone and reflect on what has happened between you and Miguel Angel. There is no loss in loss," he said. "We learn from losses. Part of loving is to learn how to let go," he added and then he left.

Walking with Papi and Mami for a few minutes in the Malecon, I was startled by the realization of love. I learn about it every day as I watch my parents, how they love each other. Mami and Papi held on to each other as they watched the ocean. I had my notebook and wrote it all down. I liked to see them loving each other as they do, and the roar of the ocean was like a song to me, like a symphony and the scent of the ocean, like an embrace, and there was nothing more beautiful to me then a Dominican sunset as the men from the Vesuvio Restaurant were setting tables for dinner. Then I felt like I was the cool-scented air. I was one with everything around me—for that one moment I was the wind, the ocean, and my parents' love. Life felt so real. I took it in, held it inside of me, and I felt a profound love for it all and I wrote it all in my notebook.

The Loss

The night was cool and I took the remnants of the newspaper Papi had left on the table the night before he died. He knew I loved to read *el Listín* and cut out poetry and news articles to place in my journal. I cut out a poem by Rafael Abreu Mejia, who speaks to me in a language I understand. I imagine I know him, this poet. I imagine that I can speak to him in a common language, that I can be open with him and call him *"tú"* instead of *"usted"*, say "Rafael" and not "Don Abreu Mejia," as if we are intimate friends.

My life is changing, and there is nothing I can do about it.

I put Rafael's poem in my journal to honor the passing of time and the fact that Rafael knows my thoughts without knowing me, understands my pain without experiencing it.

And, how does Rafael know of this place in my heart, this place that is so sad? I start to cry, and my vision is blurred as I cut out my father's obituary. Where is he right now? Is he here with us? Aura said that the dead were not gone, that they were here living their lives with us in their time. She felt death was time, that time merged in some strange multiple existence, so that my father is living in some past time while I am in my present without him. I wonder if in his time, on the other side, if he's arguing with me or if he's dancing to a Lucho Gatica song.

I read Rafael's poem.

"It is a place where suffering bleeds. It is a place made of sorrow, where memories are those hard memories, the intangibles of the body, memories without weapons (without teeth, without knives), but how they hurt, Love, how they hurt, This place love, A heavy peace, is something like the dark face of the moon. In this place love, I swear, from so much solitude, solitude dies. "

I shiver when I finish reading it. I think of this place where memories lie, and I think of Papi where he could be now, in what place his soul is sitting, reading his *Listín Diario*. Can he hear my prayer to honor his soul?

I wipe my eyes.

I walk towards my mother's bedroom to face the facts of what my life has become, one loss after the other.

A Wrinkle in the Eye

*Blessed are your eyes for they see
and your ears for they hear
(Matthew 13:16)*

It's eight thirty in the morning and Mami is in the bathtub and Julia is straightening out her bed, putting on clean sheets, cotton white sheets with hand made bordados of pink flowers. Julia flaps the sheets up and down in the air, and they smell like fresh clean laundry left out to dry in the summer breeze. This reminds me how Mami taught me to make a bed. Mami would flap those sheets up in the air like an umbrella covering the world, and life felt fresh and new again. Then she would tell me how important it was to make a bed every morning because at night, dream spirits roamed and they sent you wonderful dreams if you made your bed. Afterwards, she'd tuck the edges under the mattress and flatten out any air bubbles with the palm of her hands. A bed needed to be made perfectly; it was the way she did everything in her life. I would laugh and practice flapping the sheets, and I definitely made my bed every morning.

Now Julia puts the white cotton linen quilt with its handstitched appliqué of lilac flowers, a gently sloped green garland flanking a center medallion and the edges piped with the same green. European shams bursting with flowers, morning glories, daffodils and lilacs and other pillows of simple rose crochets and Battenberg lace decorate my mother's bed. The bed reminds me of a sanctuary. Above the bed is a picture of a short, stocky Latino man carrying a medical kit and wearing an 1930's suit. He is a modern saint, San Gregorio, from Venezuela. He comes into your dreams and either heals you or says goodbye. In my mother's dream, he said goodbye to her, and she understood that she was dying and doesn't have much time left to be with me.

When Mami started getting ill, Papi sold everything to

keep her alive and pay for her medical expenses, but soon the expenses exceeded his income. My mother's beautiful chandeliers, her antiques, and the Queen Anne table my mother so loved, and the antiques in the living room were all gone. All we have left are rocking chairs, and our beds. Julia is still with us, and she cares for us with such tenderness despite the lack of money.

Julia smiles as I enter the room. She makes the bed as my mother did when I was a child. I am fifteen years old and my mother is dying. My mother calls out my name like a question, "Mia?" Her voice is different, a little hoarse, and shaky, like that of a child who wants to cry but is trying to be brave. Julia starts to go into the bathroom to help my mother and relieve me of what I will see, but I motion for her to continue with her cleaning. I will take care of my mother. I'm sixteen now and living in the Bronx. Mami wants to die in Santo Domingo, so I am back and forth between the Bronx and the Dominican Republic.

I open the bathroom door a crack and take in a deep breath. Inhale and exhale deeply, I tell myself, and then I jump in like I would jump in at a cool pool, holding my breath tight in my chest as if by doing this I would prevent the pain of seeing the truth of what my mother has become— unrecognizable at 90 pounds. She holds on to the bars as she sits for a few minutes in a bath of roses. She is strong, my mother, even in dying.

"*Bendición, Mami,*" I say and sit on the toilet. The bathroom smells likes roses withered and pressed inside an old book.

"*Dios te Bendiga, mi'hijita,*" she says. "*Ayúdame, ven.*" She makes a slight painful motion towards getting out, and I get a fluffy soft towel to cover her and carry her out of the bathtub like she used to carry me when I was little. I look at my mother coming out of the water, holding on to the rails Papi put in the bathroom to keep her comfortable, to make life easy and dying dignified.

I feel this intense love for her and realize how much pain she is suffering, yet how strong she is in her dying. I place the towel around her, wrapping it around her body, and I notice her breasts are gone, and when I look at her face, she lowers her eyes. I can't imagine what it is like to be dying. Mami says there is nothing to fear. Death has made her humble; it has made me aware of my existence in a different way.

From afar I can hear music, *donde podré gritarte que te quiero.* Sonia Silvestre is singing that song about going to the end of the earth for her love, and I remember that the last time I heard Sonia sing, I was with Papi and Mami. I'm close to tears. I miss my father desperately. I wrap my mother and escort her to the room, watching her skinny legs, and I swallow hard for I realize how her body is slowly disappearing. I tuck her in bed, and I sit next to her on the white wicker chair. It is a warm morning. There is a silence between us in which words are not needed; we understand that this is a time of reconciliation and good-byes. I look at my mother, but she averts her eyes again. I tuck her in and make her comfortable. I sigh and I wonder if I should get into bed with her like she would with me when I was a child and afraid of the night.

She looks at me for a while in the silence, and then she says, "I had another one of those dreams."

I go to the other side of the bed, take my sandals off and get into bed with her. Mami has been having amazing dreams, pearly gates opening to light, garden dreams where there is no pain, river dreams where a boat takes her to a beautiful lake where my father is waiting for her with a bouquet of flowers.

"There is no need to fear death," she says and takes a deep breath. "There's this other side, Mia," she pauses, "it's like… the universe has a big eye that knows everything. Am I making sense?" She smiles a crooked smile.

I can never imagine my mother's losses. Having been

raised in a dictatorship where silence was the way of life and truth could cause death, she saw more than my eyes can imagine. I wish she could tell me her stories.

My mother, the one who didn't believe in anything, has begun to believe in everything. Now, she lets *las evángelicas* ladies come to the house and pray for her. When they pray it's a beautiful chant of *alabado sea el señor,* humming and whispering prayers, like a song. At night I read to her from the bible. Psalm 23 is her favorite. I take her in my arms and tuck her against my side like my father did, my breast a pillow to my mother.

Lately she speaks to me like the dead spoke through my talking board. When she is hungry she says, *"Tengo hambre por la luna"* or she tells me that *"La noche se comio el sol"* —that she's hungry for the moon and that the night has eaten the sun. I get her some fruit and she's fine. Sometimes she calls me by some other name. She tells me that I can't have her husband, that I should find my own. I tell her I will do that. *"El es mío, Mercedes, mío* and she points to her heart. She's confused me with my birth mother, the one she would not talk about. The one my father had loved so long ago and who died. The one I never met.

Today she said that the end has arrived with its wings of fire and that there is this anonymous tongue singing to the dead, "Go, look out of the window, you'll see" as if to convince me and I agree.

"Sí, Mami, sí a llegado el fin con sus alas de fuego y sí, ahi va una lengua anónima cantandole a los muertos."

My mother lives in two worlds, the world of the living and the world of the dead, and in this kind of living nothing is how it used to be. Sometimes I'm a rose, and my hands are soft petals and my breath morning dew. In the morning, she wants me to cut flowers from the imaginary thornless roses that crown on the posts of her bed.

"Can't you smell it," she'll say. I say yes, and I cut flowers I cannot see. For her my hair is water like silk, my eyes are raindrops like small diamonds, and the night is a perfumed velvet scarf with tiny holes flowing in the sky.

"I've been speaking to your father," she says to me. My heart takes a leap, for my father is dead. "Go see if your father is down in the garden," she tells me, and to indulge her, I go to the window and check, but I do not have her vision.

"You are the one who can see, Mia," she says, and I want to cry. "He's waiting for me."

She tells me how in the dream she is in the garden, and my father is there. "He gives me his hands, and he says it's going to be all right." She coughs. "So, I'm ready Mia, it's ok."

I don't answer, but just hold her.

Tears start to stream down her cheeks. I think of the past when life was easy, and I think of him walking around the house, his booming voice, the scent of Vetiver. I think of dancing those old boleros that came up on the radio on Sunday mornings when he'd take my body and swing me, and if Mami was in a good mood, he would dare to swing her around.

"I'm sorry, Mia," she says.

"Sorry? There's nothing to be sorry about."

"I wish things had been different," she says, "I would have done things differently. I would have loved more, enjoyed more, suffered less, loved you more, and I'm sorry."

"Shh, shh, shh," I say to her like a child.

I start to rub my eye, the bad left eye, the one that seems to have something stuck in it.

"What' wrong with your eyes?"

"I have a *pajita* in there, so it's bothering me, but it's ok."

She touches my eyes. "You have such beautiful eyes, Mia," she says.

"Let's see, come close," she says, and I move close to her, and I can smell the scent of roses coming out of her breath. She places her hands over my eyes to heal them so that I can see things clearly.

"Sana, Sana Culita de Rana...." She chants an old childhood healing song about a little lizard and its butt. I laugh. I never knew what a little lizard had to do with healing, but if it heals, that's ok. I hold her hand, and she says, "I will take care of you, Mia, from the other side. I promise, and you will know of me by the scent of roses, even in the winter."

She kisses my eye as if to cure all old wounds.

I laugh at this, and she places her hand on my eyes and then my heart *"Sana, Sana Culito de Rana...."* she says again.

We laugh. I kiss her hand and there is this lightness in my loving of her and all that old anger I sometimes had for her slowly disappears and is replaced by this deep longing to hold her in my arms.

The Silence of Angels
1982

Zuleika walked towards her mother's bedroom, following the singsong voices of the women on the television. Her mother, Tati, was sitting on her bed, hunched over and intent on the drama unfolding on the small set. Zuleika walked towards her, kissed her sweaty forehead, and asked for common blessings, "*Bendición, Mami.* Sorry I'm late."

"*Dios te bendiga,*" her mother responded with a voice that forgave her for everything, and she continued to watch the Spanish soap opera on Channel 47.

Zuleika glanced at the TV, staring at the dirty blonde woman in the *novela*, with her pretty light eyes and her Caucasian features; her heart shaped face and her thin little chin. Beautiful. The woman spoke in a soft, musical Spanish as her small succulent lips quivered in distress. She seemed to be on the verge, yes, on the verge of some pivotal decision that would either salvage or doom her life.

Zuleika watched in amazement as her mother began a heated discussion with the pretty woman. Tati's hand swayed like a conductor's, and she mumbled curses, imploring the woman to take the right path, "*No, por favor, no, lo hagas,*" her mother begged the woman on the tv to please not do whatever it was that she was planning to. "*Deja ese malvado,*" she continued. Her mother grew somewhat somber as she pointed at the screen with her index fingers. She told the actress the truth, her truth that happiness did not depend on a man, at least not this "*sin verguenza,*" this man without shame, or integrity, this man *sin corazón.* It was better to be alone than to make the wrong choice. Better to pass lonely nights then to lose dignity, self-respect, and *amor propio.*

"*Ay, Mami, por Dios,*" Zuleika said, laughing at her mother's seriousness. "These are just actors playing a part, just actors." Tati stared at her and responded by using a commercial break to enlighten Zuleika as to the events in the novela and why her counsel to the actress was best, and then she returned to the *tele-novela*.

Zuleika laughed. She was like a guardian angel, her mother; really she was. These thoughts reminded her of kitchen dialogues between them from years ago when her mother seriously claimed it was harder to be an angel than it was to be a human being. Angels, she would say, had to watch over you while you messed up your life, unable, and unwilling, to stop you. Her mother spoke with such conviction it almost seemed as if she owned a manual of heavenly rules and angelic regulations. She knew the ethics and protocols, the do's and don'ts of angels. She would elaborate on them at great length, certain she would impress her educated daughter with her celestial scholarship. Directly interfering with human life was against heavenly rules, her mother would say. It was unfortunate, but the angel couldn't say, "Stop! He is bad for you" or "Don't take that job, take the other one."

Zuleika once asked her mother "Then what's the use of having a guardian angel if the angel can't intercede on your behalf?" and her mother said "You must listen to the silence of angels," as if she knew the structure of their silence, the intricate details of their way of being in existence in the human world. If you listened to their silence, you will hear their messages, her mother explained, but you had to be open.

Her mother occasionally reminded her that angels also sent messages in dreams, in the synchronicities, the coincidences of life, or in those unexpected stories you hear from someone as they pass you by. You could even smell angels, her mother said. They had the dusty scent of withered roses like the ones Zuleika once found pressed in one of her grandmother's bibles back in Santo Domingo. And, their wings, she said, exuded the smoky scent of church incense. Listen. Look. Be open her mother said. "With angels, everything is *indirectas*."

Zuleika was startled from her memories by her mother's

ranting and raving over the turn of events on the tv. She stood there mesmerized by her mother's supplications. She realized her mother must be right about the angels. They did send you silent messages. For often when she made a particularly difficult decision, it had been due to an inexplicable intuition. When she went with those hunches, all went well; when she didn't, things never went as well as she had hoped. Days later she would reflect on how her intuition had tried to guide her. It was always like this, an inner voice, much wiser than she was, always sure to guide her.

Zuleika sat down next to her mother, and she looked at the wedding dress her mother had made for her. She had not wanted to think of this, and she felt her heart flutter with discomfort. Memories of her conversation with her fiancé, Paino Mejia, returned to her, but she tried to dismiss these thoughts as she sadly stared at the dress.

The wedding dress lay silently neglected on the bed. It reminded Zuleika of a woman waiting for someone to breathe life into her. Yes, a woman awaiting some kind of awakening. Zuleika sighed and stared at her mother and her strong, small hands that seem to weave magic. She wanted to clasp her mother's hands like when she was a child and cry, but she was a woman now. She had to deal with what was to come. She had to be strong. How could she tell her mother the disappointing truth? How could she break her heart, shatter her dreams, those dreams she had woven into every seam of her dress?

"God, what am I going to do?" she wondered as she thought of her fiancé's shattering revelation. He needed to explain. Oh, and how he explained. It was a mistake. A slip, he said. Men. The girl from the past, bumping into her in Santo Domingo during his Christmas visit. A warm sunny day sharing old memories and the bed invited them in. Simple. The innocent one-night stand, for old time's sake. *No significaba nada*. He wouldn't do it again. He had never done it before. *De verdad. Te lo juro*, he said as their tears mingled and she swallowed lies. Now six months pregnant, the girl was due on her wedding day. He needed her to know. He was an honest man, he said.

In the hours that followed his disclosure, she stood with him talking about his love for her, but his words seem unreal. Their wedding was in September, she reminded herself. How would she explain his dishonesty to others? Bits and pieces of their conversations would return to her, "Life goes on," he said. "Get over it." And their wedding invitations were out— too late to turn back now.

Zuleika softly touched the wedding dress. Its silkiness reminded her of things taken for granted, of children chasing white birds flying across a deep blue sky. She sighed and glanced at her mother who was still arguing with the television.

"*Ese degraciao, maldito, dejalo, dejalo,*" her mother implored. Leave him, leave that bastard; he is not good for you and will only bring you suffering," her mother told the woman in the soap opera.

"*Mami, pero, cálmate,*" Zuleika said, hoping her mother would not end up with a heart attack over the soap opera. Plus, it was hard to leave a man you loved, she told her mother, but her mother silenced her and continued watching the melodrama.

Zuleika stared tenderly at her mother and sighed with resignation as she proceeded to her bedroom. Once there she noticed how her body ached, and how heavy her head felt with thoughts and memories of her conversations with Paino. She was so tired. She took off her clothes and placed them neatly on her bed. She walked towards her bureau, brushed her hair, and pulled it back in a bun when suddenly her own pretty face startled her.

Zuleika stared at herself in the mirror as if for the first time, and the woman stared back at her with such compassion. She blinked and looked at herself again. She was amazed at how appealing her round face was. She came closer to the mirror, and observing herself, she felt an overflow of loving feelings for herself. She liked the kind shy smile that greeted her, her sweet sad eyes.

In the distance she could still hear her mother muttering to the television, but this time it was different—there was joy and relief in her mother's voice *"Gracias, Gracias, Diosito mío,"* her mother cried out for the woman in *la tele* who had finally come to her senses.

Zuleika took it all in; her mother's voice, the women in *la tele*, the view from within the mirror, the scent of roses and she laughed, and laughed, pleased with how well she was listening.

Zuleika
1984

Tati stood at the kitchen sink rolling her eyes at her daughter Zuleika and washing tomatoes, green onions and peppers for the *Asopao de Camarones* she was cooking for dinner.

"Why couldn't you lie? Why did you have to tell the truth?" Tati asked her daughter as if she had raised her to be dishonest. Zuleika tried to answer, but Tati continued confronting her with her simmering anger, spitting obscenities in between words and silences.

Zuleika was hot and sweaty, and she fanned her dress to let air cool her sweaty thighs. Tati had closed the window so that the neighbors in the building couldn't hear their argument, but as she cooked in the Bronx summer heat, the kitchen grew hotter, and the little fan on top of the old refrigerator wasn't cooling them.

"*Coño, Carajo,*" Tati said, her favored curses pursing her lips like o's in slow motion. "Now you're just a *sinvergüenza*, a woman without dignity and self respect...*y que to hizo Mariano, por Dios,* Zuleika?" she questioned, her hands a symphony of gestures as she patted them dry on her apron.

Tati took some garlic from the vegetable counter, placed the garlic cloves in the mortar, sprinkled salt, and began mashing it with a *pilón*. The sweat on Tati's forehead made her thin auburn hair frizz in the humidity like a halo above her head.

Zuleika sat quietly at the kitchen table, stripping the shrimps of their shells and cleaning them with a knife by taking off the *pupusita* in the middle, and spreading it on a napkin she kept by her side. Zuleika felt her cheeks go red, and her hands began to tremble at the thought of her husband Mariano.

"Mariano was a good man from a good family. I didn't raise you like this," Tati screamed as she pointed at Zuleika's stomach with her knife.

"*Pero, Mami...*" Zuleika tried to interrupt, but it was useless. This was one of her mother's one-way conversations and so she kept quiet.

"I raised you for better things, a family, children, *Ay Dios, dame paciencia,*" Tati said as she put the knife down and took her heart medication from the kitchen counter, the one she reserved especially for times she argued with Zuleika.

Zuleika took this opportunity to say her part.

"Mami, people get separated and divorced," Zuleika said in her most innocent of voices so as not to rouse Tati's fury even more, but she was interrupted by Tati's quick response.

"People get separated and divorced Zuleika, but you've caused a *maldito escándalo,* from the Bronx to Santo Domingo, and what do I tell the neighbors? Ah?" she said, staring at Zuleika's growing stomach.

"Ok, Mami, *pues*, I'm a little pregnant. Is that a cause for scandal?" Zuleika managed to say, and she touched her stomach with her hands.

"A little pregnant! You're a shameless cow, Zuleika, married to one man and carrying another one's child."

Zuleika inhaled and exhaled slowly, reminding herself that underneath her mother's rage was an unending love for her. She watched as Tati continued cooking and cursing and pointing at her stomach with the knife as if she were conversing with it.

Zuleika touched her stomach with the warm palm of her hands to calm the fetus inside her. She wanted to be impenetrable to harsh words and the judgment of others. Yes, she was wrong for what she did, but her child should not be the one to blame for it.

"Why couldn't you marry Paino when you had the chance?" Tati asked, "instead of going and messing around with him."

"Because...I was too young and..." Zuleika tried to finish, but felt a knot in her throat as she remembered how two years ago she had ended her engagement with Paino when he confessed his indiscretion with a woman from Santiago. He had to tell her because the woman had taken a plane straight to New York and threatened to object to the wedding. She sighed as she thought of that painful time. She had no regrets. She had ended the engagement, and she was the first person in her family to send a note of apology to the invited guests as she canceled the wedding. Her mother thought it was impulsive at the time, but she refused to marry him, and no expression of love or number of apologies could make her change her mind. A year later, she married Mariano, a childhood friend.

"Why couldn't you marry Paino when you had the chance?" Tati asked,

"I couldn't, Má, I just couldn't."

"Cause he's a *sinvergüenza* just like you," Tati said.

"Things happen, Mami."

"Sex never just happens, Zuleika," Tati said, and threw the, onions, peppers and tomatoes into the oil with garlic as the kitchen began to fill with an orgy of aromas.

"Why couldn't you use protection then?" A sensible question, but Zuleika shrugged her shoulders and played with the shrimps, which Tati snatched away in anger.

"Women…. They are so stupid nowadays," she said as she threw the shrimps into the pot. "All this protection and they don't use it. All this freedom and they find ways to be caged." She stirred the sauté, feeling very proud of herself.

"I'm free now."

"With a child and without a husband, that's what you call freedom. Hooray for liberation."

"You said a child was a blessing."

"If it's not filled with shame."

"A lie is a shame, not a child."

"I don't want to argue with you, Zuleika."

"Me neither."

"Just admit that what you did was wrong."

"I never stop admitting it, Mami."

"I feel bad. Ashamed. Don't you feel bad?"

"I don't. I have to move on, Mami. I can't stay stuck in one spot blaming myself. It's not good for me, and it's not good for the baby."

"Yeah, but how do I face the neighbors, Zuleika. What do I tell people?"

"Mami, you are a good mother. You don't owe them any explanation. My actions don't represent your goodness or your mothering."

"And the family?"

"What about the family?"

"What do I tell Tía Martirio," Tati said her eyes filling with tears. Martirio was Tati's sister, highly competitive, constantly boasting about her daughters' successes and hiding their failures and misfortunes, but gleeful over the misfortunes and losses of others. The older Tía Martirio got, the more set she was in her old ways.

"Martirio looks at me with pity in her eyes," she added.

"Ay, Mami, don't give Tía Martirio the power."

"It hurts, Zuleika, deep inside," Tati said. "Martirio looks at me with triumph. She smiles as she tells me of her daughter's new conquest, *el Americano ése come mierda* who owns the pharmacy near the university, or the fact that la *chiquita, como se llama?*

"Mimi, Mami, Mimi."

"*Que la Mimi e mierda esa* finished her university studies *en* NYU and has met *un Judió riquísimo en* New Jersey. What do I say about you—that you were married to the son of a doctor, the nephew of a general, an investment banker, and you're pregnant from Paino Mejía, *ése come mierda*?"

Zuleika sighed, "Má, please try to understand. Don't compare me to my cousins. I graduated from college, too, and I can find a job anywhere. Plus, Má, you have been a good mother, and I am a good daughter. Yes, I made a mistake for which I take responsibility. You raised me to be honest. My mistake is mine, not yours. *Y que*—does marrying

American or Jewish makes them better than me or Mia? Mami, are they better?"

"Please don't bring Mia into the conversation. She doesn't deserve at all what she got from Pito. *Ay los hombres. Dios mío. Si Trujillo tuviera vivo*, none of this would be happening. What is the world coming to? *Dios mío.*"

"*¿Mami, que tiene Trujillo que ver con esto?*" I question Trujillo, our old dictator's presence, in our conversation. What would be different if he were alive? The choices we make are ours. We should learn from our repeated mistakes.

"*Es que...,*" and she goes on to describe the need of a male presence in our family. If there were more men, she imagines the women wouldn't have to suffer so much.

"Mámi, we have to stick together. In the end we have to take responsibility for our actions and our choices. You know how Tía Martirio is."

"*Sí, sí.*"

"She likes to create division. I don't even think she understands what she does. She'll come here to brag about one thing or another, and I have nothing to brag about. We've made some mistakes, and we are trying to live good lives . I still love Mariano, Mami. He understands me better than anyone in the world. We are still good friends, even though we are separated. Please, let's not act like to marry a white man is more important than to marry a Latino."

"*Pero, Zuki, e que son uno desgraciado, sinvergüenza, mujeriegos sin valores.*"

"Not all of them, Má, there are good Latino men out there."

Tati stood silent in front of the stove.

"*Es verdad, coño, carajo,*" she said.

"It's true," Zuleika repeated.

"*Sí, sí,*" Tati said. They started bad mouthing Tía Martirio and bonded again through local gossip and after a few laughs, Tati turned the situation around to blame Mariano.

"*Eso e una mujercita*," adding that Mariano had another woman.

"*Es mi culpa*," Zuleika said and lowered her eyes knowing the truth. "*No es la del*," she added defending him.

"*Na, Una mujercita*," she said as she cleaned the counter with a burgundy towel "You know that *another woman* is no reason to leave your husband."

"Ay, Mami." Zuleika smiled.

"It's true, men have mistresses all of the time, but the mistresses, they have a short life span. You wait and see. Mistresses are like the glue on a cheap envelope—the more you lick it, the less it sticks."

Zuleika laughed.

"*Te lo digo*," Tati said and they laughed together.

By now the fishy scent of the *Asopao* permeated the house, and it reminded Zuleika of Santo Domingo and Mariano. At night she dreamed of his smile, the way he held her at night. Sometimes she wished she was back there with him, but their actions had turned her life around, changed their destiny. Maybe she should not have listened to her cousin Eva, who was the first to raise her suspicions or to her best friend, Rica, who suggested that Zuleika keep an eye on Mariano. She ignored it at first. She thought Rica was jealous of Zuleika's newfound happiness in her marriage. Rica had married Estanly, her childhood boyfriend in Santo Domingo, and they had four girls in search of that boy that would carry his name, but when he couldn't find it with Rica, he had no problem searching out other women. Rica sought to soothe her disappointments in her old love of women, particularly Zuleika.

One night Rica made a sexual advance to Zuleika as they talked about the past, friends and lovers. She recalled how Rica's lips came close to hers and pressed themselves softly as they had done many years ago when they were adolescents. Rica's hands softly entered her blouse and touched her breast, but Zuleika resisted. Rica reminded her that loving a woman was not the same as having an affair with a man. Mariano would understand. Zuleika laughed, for her sex was sex, with a man or a woman.

"But there are women who have sex with women and don't consider themselves lesbians , and there are many men out there who have sex with men and don't consider themselves gay," Rica said.

But that wasn't the problem. If she had wanted Rica, she would have fulfilled her desires, but to use her sexually because she was a woman and to consider an affair with her less than an affair didn't seem right to Zuleika. "An affair is an affair with a man or a woman," Zuki thought, and she was very happy with Mariano.

Despite the rejection, and in between soft touches, Rica pressed her concerns. Wasn't she worried about Mariano and his buddies always hanging out in the summer house? Zuleika thought about this for some time. It was true that he spent hours in the summerhouse, but their relationship was filled with love and honesty. He was always there for her, had so much to share with her, and their lovemaking was effortless and passionate. There was no reason to suspect a mistress. Rica continued to touch Zuleika. Zuleika felt her body blend into Rica's yearning, the warmth of Rica's desire traveling through her, leaving her limp with satisfaction. Afterwards, Zuki told Rica that they could not kiss again, that it wasn't right for them or for her marriage. Rica promised, but before they ended the night, Rica suggested Zuleika pop up to the summerhouse unannounced one evening to see what kind of women visited.

Then one night without telling Rica, Zuleika drove unannounced to the summerhouse, her stomach tight, her chest heaving, her armpits sweating. She was glad she went alone. She entered the summerhouse, took off her shoes, and felt the coolness of the cement floor. She could smell the salty scent of the ocean and crushed flowers that had fallen out of the potpourri bowl onto the floor. She picked them up and placed them on the table. Clothes were strewn over the white wicker furniture, the *Listín Diario* was spread open on the floor, and empty plates and cups littered the dining room table. She stood there in the house like a ghost, unable to move, glued to the floor. Her heart beating fast, her breath short and shallow, she managed to walk to the master bedroom. Her hands trembled as she opened the door to her room, and there she saw them. Sleeping.

Dios mío, she said to herself as she saw her husband clearly, curled spoon like against Carlos' strong, muscular body. Carlos was an interior decorator from Arroyo Hondo known for his bisexuality and seduction of married men, but he was her best friend, and she had trusted him. Here he was in deep sleep, mouth open wide, snoring, and they were in her bed, covered only by the bone-white of the moonlight.

Zuleika took a deep breath and swallowed. Her throat was dry and she wanted to weep, but she was mute, frozen. She wanted to hurt something, or someone, but then her body was taken by a deep urge to have Mariano inside of her, so deep inside of her that his penis floating in her would be hers forever, and he would have nothing left for Carlos. Instead she ran out of the house, tripping on the white wicker furniture and breaking a lamp. When she arrived home, she called Paino, who immediately came to her.

It was true that she had acted foolishly by making love to Paino, but she couldn't think of anything but her need to be comforted. So she held on to him as she had done years ago when she first met him and without words they made love.

Tati startled Zuleika from her memories, "I'm sorry, Zuleika, I shouldn't be treating you this way in your condition,"

"It's ok, Má."

"*Quiere tostones?*"

"Sure, What's an *Asopao* without *tostones?*"

Zuleika loved the soupy consistency of the *Asopao*. The vegetable, rice, and shrimps were little treasures one could find in a mouthful. She loved it with fried green plantains and an avocado salad.

Tati opened the kitchen window to let in some fresh air and took two green plantains from the vegetable counter. With the skill of a Sushi Chef she striped each of them of their thick green covering. They lay motionless on the surface of the wooden table, like a man's erect penis, and she skillfully sliced them into perfectly neat quarters and placed them carefully on the hot boiling oil in the frying pan. After frying them for about ten minutes, she took them out, flattened them, fried them again, and then let them cool, sprinkled with salt.

¿*Como Se Dice* Success in Spanish?
1986

Mia sat on Tati's bed and shuffled the Tarot cards on the white Chenille bedspread and then picked them up to shuffle them again. It was a three card spread, the present, the past and the future.

In the distance Tati was cooking an *habichuela con dulce,* and the overheated apartment smelled of sweet potatoes, beans, raisins, cloves and cinnamon sticks. Mia closed her eyes as she shuffled the cards and whispered a question while Zuki watched.

"I just want to see what the future holds. Did I make the right decision in leaving him?"

"Mia leaving is not an easy decision, but usually it is a good decision." Zuki said.

"Look at you, you left Mariano, went back and now you are happy. Not only did love triumph above all, but your mistake was forgiven."

"Things were not as they seemed," Zuki said and then added "It's different Mia, Pito left when you most needed him,"

"No, I left him because I am happier without him."

"Well, I think he was wrong. You have been the most faithful person. He didn't have to question you," Zuki said as she looked at Mia's growing stomach. "I think he judged you because of me."

"Please Zuki, don't blame yourself for my situation. I should have known better. The signs of his infidelity were there. He just needed an excuse to feel good about leaving me."

Mia shuffled the cards and then spread them like a fan on the bed and picked three.

"Here," she said as she handed it to Zuki.

Zuki placed the cards on the bed and said, *"Tu presente,*

tu pasado, y tu futuro," as she placed each one of the Tarot cards faced down.

The first card was the card of death, represented by a skeleton dressed in a black robe and carrying a scythe."

"This is the card of transformation and new beginnings."

"Good because I don't want to suffer for men anymore," Mia said. "I want to be strong, to let go when it is time to let go and to stay and work hard when it is time to stay,"

"That's good because you deserve the best, Mia."

"We all do. I want love that is not painful and dramatic."

"Is there such a thing?"

"Yes, life will have challenges, Zuki, in the bag of good apples there will be some rotten ones that look good on the outside, but we need to know what we tolerate and what we don't. When to leave and when to stay. "

"Ok, lets continue, *tu pasado,"* Zuki said as she picked up the second card. "The ten of wands,"

Mia looked at this card. She never liked it. It always represented "struggle" and "oppression". The card depicted a sad man carrying ten heavy poles that were weighing him down.

"Your Past," Zuki said as she went on to describe the meaning of the card, oppression, struggle. Mia thought of the past, of her life with Pito.

After her parents' death, Mia arrived to the Bronx to live with relatives. After a bitter fight among relatives over who would raise Mia, Tati won out, and Mia moved her belongings from Tía Martirio's apartment to Tati's. Thank God, Mia thought, and praised the Lord. The twelve years of Balaguer's regime was over and a new president had been elected. Most of her Bronx friends were returning from Santo Domingo to the United States, but she soon lost touch with them. Rica returned pregnant, and she soon petitioned Estanly as she had promised. Upon his arrival, they married, moved in with her mother until they found an apartment in the building.

On her way to school one early morning, Mia bumped into Pito. They quickly caught up with the events of their lives. They had met in Junior High, and now here she was almost graduating from high school and thinking about college. A few months later they became a couple. Mia saw him every day and he became the fiber that wove a structure into her life. On Fish Fry Friday's they met at Rica's apartment. Rica's father, *el Doctor*, supervised the household with a hand of steel. He'd make sure no one was having sex, let along unprotected sex. He'd come into the apartment unexpectedly and untangle everyone from their embraces, praising God and quoting the bible, and he'd leave ranting and raving.

Mia often thought that *el Doctor,* with his old desire for children and his bad love for Rica, should not be part of their lives. He should go somewhere far off with his lack of memory and his saintly verses. And Estanly, he didn't deserve to be part of their world, but there he was, the father of Rica's child and a constant in their lives. At least he, like *el Doctor*, had forgotten much, and not once did he remind her of the past, not once did his lips try to touch hers, and not once did he tell Pito about their old love. Rica, too, had suppressed her memory and never spoke of the faint lines on her wrist from the time when she would rather have died than not have Estanly, back then when he tried to leave her to be with Mia. They never spoke of these things.

On those Fridays, in Rica's little overheated apartment, they would remember their days in Santo Domingo. In Rica's apartment, the boleros and merengues would soothe their longing for the love of their homeland and the memories of those they left behind. The faces of her old friends were soon replaced by new faces—Papo, El Turco, La Blanqui, Tony, Manny and Pito. Eva would leave her baby with her parents and come for an hour or two. She was in love with Papo, and they would spend breathless hours in a corner, their lips glued to each other. Mimi and Rosa would fight with Tía Martirio, who would threaten to disown them if they defied her, and whose tough love approach was to lock the door with an extra lock and leave them out in the hallway for a few minutes until she tired of hearing them knock.

Tati allowed Pito to visit Mia and accepted their relationship. So, Mia and Pito did everything together, disco parties and apartment parties. They were not allowed to go out of the confines of the Bronx, so everything they did, they did in the Bronx, shopping at the Hub on 149th St. or Fordham Road and dancing in the streets. They were not allowed to go on weekends, sleep in anyone's home, or stay over at their boyfriends' homes. Still, Pito was patient.

On the weekends, Pito and Mia visited tourist sights, the Statue of Liberty, The Cruise Line, Tribeca, the Twin Towers, and the top of the Empire State Building, and they would have dinner in China Town or watch a movie on 42nd Street and then go for a steak with potatoes. Mia loved to sway among the moving New Yorkers, oblivious to her presence, and in her enormous love for Pito; Mia blessed everyone that passed by. Pito would often kiss the palm of her hand as he led her to cross the streets. His hand on her hand, guiding her, protecting her. When Pito said he loved her, it always confirmed that life was good and that she was on the right track. He became her friend, her lover, her mother and her father. She tried to enjoy every minute knowing that it may not last forever. Mia completed college, and Pito joined the police force. Soon Pito and Mia found a small apartment in the building and they moved in together. The family was not pleased, "If you move in with him, it's over, he'll never marry you," they would all say.

Pito would remind her that they didn't need a piece of paper to demonstrate their love, plus they had been together longer than any of their friends' marriages and friendships. It didn't take long after they moved in together for Pito to feel restless. He felt confined. Suffocated. He hated this idea of living together, of marriage. He didn't like the responsibilities. His job was demanding. Soon the arguments began. Pito was never pleased with anything Mia did. Mia was never pleased with his late night outs. The more she complained the more he needed to assert his authority.

Soon, his job kept him away from her for days and night. When he returned, she did not recognize him. He was distant, irritable and uncommunicative. At night, she'd wait for him on the windowsill to catch a glimpse of him entering the building, but the hours would pass and the roar of the L train would bring tired bodies from a late night out, but not her Pito. She wondered if it was all about work. She would worry and then become jealous and then feel guilty when he mentioned the dangers of his job.

After years of questioning and asking where he'd been and where he's going, Mia found the strength to let him go. It wasn't easy. By then Mia had come to the conclusion that learning to live included learning to let go. She'd been with Pito longer than with anyone in her life. If love had an expiration date, this relationship was past its due date. It didn't take long after leaving him that she found out she was pregnant. When she tried to call him to speak to him, he wouldn't return her calls. He was angry that she left.

Finally, one day as she was walking on the Grand Concourse, she bumped into him around Fordham Road. She told him she was pregnant and she noticed he was not happy.

"*¿Y es mío?*" he asked, knowing how deep the question would hurt her. She had nothing to say. Those words echoed in her head and seem to take away the little bit of love she had left in her for him. She had no explanations to give. When she tried to speak words did not come out. Then, as they were about to say goodbye, a distinguished Dominican man that reminded her of her father, came to happily greet Pito.

"*Hola*, Pedro," the older man said with great joy and pride in his voice, calling Pito by his birth name.

He wore the same Vetiver cologne as her father and a

Chacavera shirt just like him. He was tall, regal and dignifided. When Pito called him Don Mellon, she knew he had to be a man of importance. Then the man looked at her, questioning her presence and looking at her growing stomach, and then at Pito.

She stood there in front of this man who was someone's father, and she gave him her hand. His was a warm kind hand. The kind of hand that would care for a daughter like her and not let anything happen to her. But, she was alone in the world with no one to protect her, but herself. She noticed Pito's sweat on his forehead and his sudden reaction.

"This is my cousin, Ynoemia."

Mia was stunned, full of pain and disbelief. She felt dizzy and the image of the older man seemed distant. His voice echoing in the distance as he told Pito, *"Hay que hacer las preparaciones,"* that preparations needed to be made. Preparations for what? she wondered. She started to sweat and felt nauseous and the older man noticing her discomfort came to her aide, "Are you ok," he questioned. She apologized and said she had to go. They said their good-byes, and Ynoemia looked at Pito who had lowered his eyes. He had nothing to say. He had no explanations to give. She could not breathe, it was as if her heart had grown dead inside of her. Pito had lied in the past, but not like this, and not in front of her. She felt desperately alone. She wanted to cry, to speak, to scream, but she could not act. She walked away and sat on the steps of a building and cried.

Zuki coughed and summarized the last two Tarot cards before proceeding.

"The Present is represented by the card of death symbolizing transformation, the past is symbolized by the ten of wands, representing oppression and the future. Mia is represented by the Lovers."

Mia smiled as she looked at the Lovers. She knew that her future would be filled with love and stability. Her unborn child was a gift from heaven that would bring her to a place of joy and peace.

Zuki picked the card of the lovers up. "Here is Adam and Eve with a tree, serpent and apples. Adam is joyful, he's found a soul mate and he's content. A new love is coming your way. You are going to fall in love. There is success."

"I'm pregnant, Zuki, who is going to want me?"

"I'm just the messenger, Mia."

Tati came in curious as to the events of Mia's destiny.

"What's in the cards?"

"Success,"

Tati stared at Mia and then at Zuki to translate.

"*¿Que es* success?" Tía Martirio asked.

Mia was silent. She hated it when she forgot a word in Spanish.

"¿Zuki, *como se dice* 'success' in Spanish?"

"Success?"

Tati was not fluent in English, but tried to be, so she said "Suck-Sex,"

"Success, Má, success, no suck sex, *eso no es bueno*," Zuki said.

"*Eso es suseso?*" Tati asked.

"No, no, *successo* es incident in English."

"*Oh, pero es success algo malo?*".

"No, nothing bad, Tía."

Mia went to her bookshelf and looked up "Success" in the Spanish English dictionary.

"There. Success means, *Exito*."

"*Exito,*" they all said.

Exito, Mia thought, *Exito* was a great word for success. *Exito* sounds like Exit in English. Mia thought of *Exito*, she thought of X, and Ex's, the things one ends or takes out of one's life, the things one leaves behind no matter how attached one is. To Mia that meant success. To be able to know when to stay and when to leave. To have the courage to live beyond loss. To have the courage to say, I will go on. They laughed, and Zuki said, "Exito."

"You know that a woman needs to learn to be on her own," Mia said and she added, "You can say love sucks, you know, but it sucks because you want it to suck, but love can be beautiful, love can be peaceful. Love does not kill or cause pain. Love does not control or tell me how I must be or what to wear or when I can cut my hair. Love allows me to be who I am. Love doesn't have to be drama and other women with your man's baby. Love doesn't have to be that way. Love can be powerful. Love can heal. Let's promise ourselves we will try hard to have a good life, Zuki, with men or without them."

There was hope for the future. She could raise her child on her own and find love eventually. She took the cards and placed them together in their pouch and thanked Zuki for the reading and they stood up and followed Tati to the kitchen to the sweet scent of *habichuela con dulce*, as Tati asked Mia again, *¿Y como es que se dice* success in Spanish?"

Casa-Arte
for J. B.

Spring 1986

Mia walked toward the old Victorian house with its gingerbread trimming. The house was pink and lavender and stood out from the hills to make a statement. Her cousin Zuleika and her husband, Mariano had bought the house at a moderate price in Tarrytown. Around it were scented Magnolias whose purple and white petals lay on the ground.

As Ynoemia entered, she could hear the voices coming from sitting room and caught the smell of herbs emanating from the kitchen. Zuki's daughter was learning to walk and Tati was close behind her.

"*Bendición, Tia.*"

"*Hola, mi hija,*" Tati said, and they kissed.

Mia spoke about how big the child was. She was awed at the miracle of growth. Mia touched her own belly hoping that all went well with her pregnancy. She was six months pregnant and a single parent.

Zuki's daughter was learning to walk, and Tati caught her.

"The house is beautiful, Zuki. You and Mariano have done an amazing job." Zuki kissed her on both cheeks like Mariano loved to do. It suddenly struck Mia that time was passing quickly. Zuki was all grown up and the head of a household. Mariano came running from upstairs in his unique way, making an entrance and screaming her name.

"*Mia, querida!*" he yelled and coming from his handsome lips, her name sounded like a foreign language. Mariano was working with a television station. On the side he played with film and photography. Recently, he had sold black and white photos of Zuki's naked body when she was pregnant. Tati was appalled. "*Es arte, Mami,*" Zuki had told her.

"Mariano, *mi amor,*" Mia said and praised him for the work in the house. "It's gorgeous,"

"A labor of love," he said and added, "You are going to love this event and there is someone I want you to meet."

A friend was performing a dance called Casarte. It was symbolic meditation, a story in movement. A collage of silent words."

Suddenly, Zuki came with a wooden spoon in hand and asked Mariano to taste her Penne Vodka sauce, and he did.

"*Delicioso.*"

Mariano hugged her and urged Mia to get comfortable. "*Ésta es tu casa,* Mia."

The house was filled with people, comfortably talking to each other. They were all Zuki's friends. No one she knew. She said hello to everyone and from a far she could spot a handsome young man who reminded her of Santo Domingo. The baby kicked in her stomach and she touched it. She could feel the tip of the baby's elbow. She laughed, the miracle of birth didn't stop amazing her.

She sat next to the handsome young man who reminded her of the past. It was the way his curly hair fell on his forehead and how sweetly he smiled at her when she looked over. Then the man glanced at her and said, "*Hola.*"

She sat down, looked at his portfolio and then at him. "I am always amazed at the ability to create new things. How it is that poets, writers, and artists come up with ideas?"

"Are you an artist?" He asked.

"I'm not sure," she lied. "I like to create art. It's not like I have a degree in creating art. So, I'm not sure what that makes me. I use art for healing, though, I'm a social worker. Art heals."

"I'm a social worker too, you know. HIV unit at the Veteran's Hospital."

"South Side Community Mental Health. Near Lebanon Hospital in the Bronx."

"Very interesting. This is such a coincidence," he said. "What kind of art do you do?"

"I create collages, cut pieces up and paint them with acryclic."

"You are an artist, say it."

She laughed, but couldn't get herself to say it. Art. She made collages and in all of them was her father cut up in little pieces and buried in acryclic paint so that no one but her could find him. Creating was like being possessed by a spirit, it was sacred and holy, for the ideas and the process came from somewhere that was nameless—that is how she saw it. So she shared this with him and he listened attentively.

"I would love to see your collages," he said.

"Sure," she answered quickly. She could imagine they would go to dinner or visit a museum. Would she make love to him? Would he want to make love to her? She laughed. He stared at her.

"But enough about my process, tell me about you?"

He spoke of his favorite authors, painters, and poets, and laughed as they found similarities in their love of art, literature and social work.

"How did you end up here?"

"I know Mariano from Santo Domingo. I met him there once in Altos *de* Chavon. I studied there."

"Oh."

"I'm here because of the Casarte. Mariano invited me."

"Have you seen Elena before?"

"Yes, I love her," he said and Mia wondered if he was with Elena. "She's like a sister to me," he added. "It all started with an apartment, so she called it "Apart - Arte""

"Apartarte, for apartment and art?"

"Yes, yes."

"Apartarte also means to separate."

"Yes, but what happened was that Mariano asked her to do it here, and she couldn't say Apartarte because this is a big old Victorian house. So, she changed the name of the event to Casa Arte."

"Interesting because Casa Arte is Casarte and that means 'to marry.'"

"Yes."

Mia wanted to share with him her desire for a partner who would allow her to create, who wouldn't see her creativity as a threat, but as a blessing that would enhance the partnership. As she thought of marriage, the baby in her tummy kicked again. She soothed the fetus with the palm of her hand.

She listened while he spoke, but she was lost in the sweet scent of him. He had the smell of Santo Domingo, of mangos, and papayas being sold in the hot sun, of the wet earth after an afternoon shower and the roaring ocean in el Malecon. She liked something about his essence. She felt giddy and laughed at herself because she thought she would never feel anything for anyone. She noticed he had an art portfolio next to him and some art books. "I would love to see your portfolio, if you don't mind,"

"No, please," he said and placed it in between the chair that separated them. Then he took the portfolio from the chair and asked her to sit next to him. Her heart filled with joy as she felt the baby kicking again when he said, "Sit closer."

"Thanks," she said and took the portfolio and opened it. She sensed his face close to hers, his head brushing hers as they stared down at the portfolio. She had not been this close to a man since the last time she made love to Pito. Deep inside she missed a man's touch, the warmth of his kisses.

"This is beautiful," she said as she was drawn to his bold colors and surrealist expression of his dreams.

"My dreams are an inspiration," he said.

"So are mine."

From afar she noticed a woman was looking at them, and she wondered if she was with him. God, she hoped he was alone at the party. He actually never mentioned a woman. The woman came close enough to look at the portfolio. Ynoemia ignored her.

When she finished with the portfolio, he put it on his lap and handed her a small book the size of her hand like a codex she'd seen in a bookbinding class. The book told a story in pictures all created by him. She longed to know more about him. She was awed by his paintings. As a child she wished to paint and draw, but her father considered the life of an artist promiscuous and wouldn't allow it. But now that her father was gone and she was a woman, she didn't care very much for what others thought, and she could do what she wanted.

"This is great," she said and smiled at him and he returned the smile.

They chatted a while. She was pleased that he, like her, was a social worker. He worked at the Veteran's Hospital in the AIDS unit. He was also an artist, a book artist. He drew, and painted, and made books. He was so right.

"That is so wonderful," she said.

"Thanks."

"You know what is wonderful about life is that you can do whatever you want, you know. You can play the piano and be a doctor. You can write poetry and knit. You can be a chef and a singer. You can be whatever you want."

"That's so funny. I was thinking about that this morning," he said and she noticed he looked at her stomach and then her ringless fingers.

"Where's the father?"

"I left him," she said

"A good choice?"

"A good one, but not an easy one."

"It takes a lot of courage to do that."

She remained silent.

"What kind of relationship was it?... I hope you don't mind my asking,"

"No, no. It was like any other relationship. It started good," she said. Yes, he was good, she thought, he served a purpose in my life when I had lost everything.

"Time passes and everything changes. How do you deal with love and the passing of time? Love is hard work."

"I know what you mean. The same happened to me."

"Really?"

She sensed a deep sadness in him. Who would have known, she thought, that she would bump into a normal guy in a performance called *Casarte*.

"What is your name?" she asked, realizing that they had not introduced each other.

"*Ay perdón, perdón.* My name is Roberto Ross from the Rosses in Sosua. Born in the Dominican Republic, Puerto Rican-Dominican parents with a Jewish heritage neither of them remember, and raised in the Bronx.

"*Y usted, cómo se llama?*"

"*Tú*, please *tú*... we've shared too much to be *usted*, don't you think?"

"Ok, ok...*y tú, cómo te llamas?*"

"My name is Ynoemia, but you can call me Mia. I was born in Santo Domingo to Dominican parents. I was raised in the Bronx."

"Great...a Bronx girl in Tarrytown, New York."

"Where do you live?"

"In the Bronx, but soon I'll move up here," she said to give him hope.

They laughed, and she felt a growing comfort with him.

A young woman with a strong presence that reminded her of her cousin Eva brushed against Mia as if she were invisible and sat next to them. She was tall, with tight-fitting jeans and high heels and an old tattered jacket. Her hair was long and curly and smelled like herbal essence. She was bold and honest with a hoarse voice, and looked at Roberto and said, "Great work."

"*Gracias*."

She'd been watching it from across the room and wanted to take a closer look. He handed her the portfolio.

"*Eres Chavonero*," the woman said as she leafed through the portfolio. He smiled with pride at the fact that she recognized his art as that kind that came from an artist colony known as *Altos de Chavon* in La Romana.

"*Sí, soy Chavonero*," he said and acknowledges that he had studied at *Altos de Chavon*. They spoke quickly in between laughter and recognition and ignored her presence in the middle. Mia remained quiet because she wanted things to flow. She could have stopped the interchange, but she wanted to let it be. The woman extended her long brown arm towards him, hitting Mia on her face and did not think once to apologize.

Mia looked at this woman. She had nice light brown skin, and her layered hair fell down in cascades across her pretty face. Her eyes were wide and bright, but they were not focused on her as much as they were on him. Mia stared at him and then at her and fell like a spectator at a tennis show, looking right, left, and right. Mia watched as the young woman introduced herself and offered her services.

"Veronica, *a su servicio*."

"*Yo soy Roberto*," he said

"*Mucho gusto,*" she replied and went on about how glad she was to meet a *Chavonero*. It was the first time Mia heard of such a term and she was pleased with how Dominicans made up words. She loved that about them, that and their sense of humor, and popular phrases. The woman asked what year he attended.

"*Clase del ochenta-tres,*" she said.

"*Y yo soy clase del ochenta-cinco*," he replied and commented that they had missed each other by a year.

"You know...and....and..." and she mentioned a few artists

from the colony. *"Esos Chavonero"* she said, and they laughed the kind of laughter that placed them in a special group of people—unique, creative, and somehow above it all.

Mia listened quietly looking around and observing all of the artists and non-artists at the house. God she wished she had a group of some kind that she could belong too, where people were kind to each other. A group where she could say, *"Soy Chavonera,"* like she really belonged.

"Siéntate aqui," she said to the woman, getting up, and the woman quickly sat in her chair, almost tripping her in the process without a "thank you" for the offer. Instead she continued talking to Roberto without once looking at her or acknowledging her presence. Ynoemia thought of Eva who would say that she was really stupid, but Mia looked at her growing stomach and thought it was ridiculous to even have these thoughts about this man. She reminded herself that she would no longer make mistakes, that she would not be involved in relationships that were not productive.

La Verónica spoke about this *Chavonero* and that Chavonero in her beautiful Dominican singsong Spanish. Mia envied her freedom, her fluidity. She spoke about everything and didn't take a break, so when Roberto found a pause in which to stop the woman from speaking and he said, "Can I please introduce you to my friend, Mia,"

"Oh," the woman said as if she just realized that there was another woman there. *"Mucho gusto."*

"Mucho gusto," Mia said and they shook hands.

"Where were we?" Veronica asked him.

Mia took a sigh and decided to get away from it all. Mia walked towards the table to find comfort in food. She looked back for a moment and saw how Roberto coughed, looked at his watch, apologized, and said, *"Mucho gusto en conocerte, Verónica."* He walked towards the table where Mariano and Zuleika had placed fruits, cheese and crackers.

From a distance, Mia noticed that Mariano was making

some strange sign language as he pointed to Roberto and whispered to Mia, "he's the one," and then Mia realized that Roberto was the person Mariano wanted her to meet.

Roberto stood before her and said, "Mariano has been trying to get us to meet for the longest time," he waved at Mariano. Mia looked at him and then at Roberto and she wondered about the timing. Here she was pregnant and meeting a man. Her baby fluttered inside of her. She was hungry. Intuitively, he picked an apple for her.

"Do you see this apple?"

"Yes."

"This apple has been completed misunderstood throughout history, just like women. Don't you think?" he questioned and he handed the apple to her.

The baby moved again as she took the apple and a flow of joy passed through her. She smiled and took the apple from his hand.

My Daughter's Eyes
2000

My daughter Gabriela assaults me with a Maybeline eyeliner. Her hands are trembling; I suppose she's nervous because she's taking a risk by asking me to do her eyes. I know she's afraid I'll disagree with the eyeliner thing, but I know, too, that if I disagree, I'll give the eyeliner more value than it has.

The Maybeline eyeliner has not changed much since I was thirteen. It is still a thin red pencil the size of my middle finger. My cousins and I used to place the tip of it in fire to make it melt so the line on our eyelids would be thick and dark, Latina style, but my eyes were too small, and the dark lines would threaten to overwhelm them. Back then, my cousins and I weren't allowed to wear makeup, no lip gloss, no eye shadow, and no eyeliner.

My cousin Eva, our best friend America, and I would make up our eyes on 170ᵗʰ Street and Grand Concourse on our way to the D train to Wade Junior High. Eva looked great when she did her eyes like Cleopatra, because her eyes were large and violet like Elizabeth Taylor's, and she was short and shapely just like Elizabeth, and she had that same little Taylor face, and so when she did her eyes the guys would whistle at her. When we arrived at the school, my homeroom teacher, Ms. Rodriguez would have this miserable face every time she saw me looking like a raccoon, "You don't need all of that makeup, Mia, you look beautiful without it," she'd say and brush it off. I used to love Ms. Rodriguez. I liked it that she became a mirror to my beauty. It was later when she became concerned about my playing hooky with the Dragon Slayers that she called my parents and reported my absences at Wade Junior High. She had no idea of the devastation she would create.

It's November and it's early in the morning and I've just finished my morning meditation facing east where the sun rises. Today, I imagined that the beams of the sun were God's rays bringing me peace and comfort. I work as a social worker with sexually abused children, and it is not an easy job.

I look at my daughter's eyes. They are green. A dusty green and against her pale skin, they look very light. This reminds me of the first time her father saw her and he said, "She doesn't look like me at all."

"It's just a little bit, mom."

"I'm not sure about this."

"Why?"

"You're just thirteen," I say and argue about her age and the months and days until she turns fourteen.

"Ok, thirteen and a half," I say.

"Good, here," she says and hands the eyeliner to me

I hold onto the Maybeline eyeliner, and its feel reminds me of the past, when I was young and wanted to be loved and to belong.

Gabi's done her hair straight in the Dominican Salon on Beekman Avenue in Sleepy Hollow and under the glow of the morning light I see strands of gold highlights. Gabi has been sneaking around with her cousins in the Bronx and lightening her hair with hair mousse that leaves it over-bleached and dry like straw, but today, after a Dominican conditioner, it is silky-smooth and straight, and she looks just like who she wants to look like—her idol, Jennifer Lopez.

I look around, and I think of Jennifer who has taken over my house. Jennifer's pictures are everywhere—over the mantel on the fireplace; in the dining room, stuck on the corner of the mirror next to the picture of my ex-husband and best friend in the world, pasted on walls and doors. On our refrigerator door her lips are puckered up in tiny O's as she sings, her image frozen in time next to my magnetic poetry that says:

Luscious, Tongue

Suck, Love

Purple, Sunset

Orange Spices

Jennifer has been trimmed into four by fours and neatly placed in trendy frames from Kmart. She smiles at us as if she were a friend or relative, her photo there in our living room, sharing with us our joy and sorrows. Gabi and I talk about Jennifer as if we know her. I wonder about her leaving Sean Puffy combs, a.k.a. Puff Daddy, now P. Diddy, and getting married too soon. I could've told her it doesn't work. I am sure her mother did, but she didn't listen.

Now, from her previous mistakes I can see the next ones to come, that she will leave her present husband in a matter of a few months because she didn't leave any transition to go from one love to another. It is the mistake so many women make, including me. Gabi and I seem to bond as we talk about JLo and her mistakes and her successes, JLo's life mirroring choices of my own, mistakes all women I know have made, transitions they've not allowed themselves to have, and so they move on to the next lover with the wound still bleeding, with the gap, with the hole. I hope Gabi doesn't make those mistakes, yet I know that I cannot protect her from men. I can tell her stories to guide her, but in the end, she will make her own choices. I will have to sit and watch. I can make an herbal recipe to avoid love disaster. I can pray for her to meet a good man who will respect her, but in the end I cannot control the events in her life. She makes her own choices, just like I made mine. I am sure JLo's mother has cried and cringed at the mistakes JLo has made, but there was nothing she could do. All she could do is wait to see the next move and hope that JLo learned her lesson.

We are standing in the living room in front of the fireplace. I notice that my husband, Roberto, has left me an apple with a note, a reminder of his love for me. The thought of him and his symbolic request to be loved reminds me of how lucky I am, but as the warm feeling of love for my husband surfaces, Gabi startles me, reminding me of her request. The Maybeline eyeliner staring at me like a weapon that will separate or unite my daughter and me.

"I don't know Gabi," I say as I look at the Maybeline eyeliner.

"Mommy, please. Everyone does a little bit of makeup."

"No, it's just that your eyes, they are so pretty without eyeliner. This will ruin it all." I say weakly.

"No, it won't. Nothing will happen."

"Promise."

"Pinky promise."

My daughter tilts her face towards me, and I wonder what is in her head. Who is she trying to please? I stretch the end of her closed eye to make the eyelids tight like a palette, and then I press the tip of the eyeliner and create a smooth line. I feel as if I am writing a story on her eyelid. I hear the inner voices of my parents telling me not to do it. Ynoemia, you'll regret it, the voices say to me. The dead speaking to me, warning me about the future. There definitely has to be a boy, a voice says, and boys ruin it all. Suddenly, the boy will become more important than our relationship. She will defy me and run off with him. No, I say to the voices. This is my daughter. I raised her to be a loyal person, to love her family above all. Men. They'll influence her to go against you. Don't do it, an inner voice says.

Suddenly, I remember when she was three. There was no guilt then when I did her eyes for Halloween and saw the awe in her face when I painted her tiny fingernails blue. But now I'm afraid for her, afraid of how she will be perceived when she goes to the *colmado* and grown men high on beer say to her, *"Mami, pero qué cuerpazo"* without realizing the fear this creates in her.

My heart flutters.

Anxiety, the strange way in which my body speaks to me, alerting me, telling me to be careful. I decide not to let the voices of the past separate us. This is my daughter, the one who loves me and says, "Let me take care of you, Mommy, like you've taken care of me" when my Lupus flares up and I cannot breathe, when my joints swell and I am exhausted.

I move her face from one side to the other, and I step back to see her clearly as if she were a canvas that was coming alive. Her eyes remind me of the past. As I look in them, my life plays like a movie in them. I think of my father. I think of my mother. Mami and Papi would never have approved. I think of them, and I wish they were here, that their strength would make me strong.

"This should be just for parties," I say.

"Uh huh," she mutters as I continue.

"For special occasions."

She agrees.

"My mother would never allow it," I say finding my strength.

"I'm sure," she responds.

"Just a smear," I say, as if speaking to the other eye, and I press the eyeliner ever so slightly on the eyelid barely making an impact and then I say, "Ok, done."

Gabi runs towards the mirror in the living room, the one next to the door, and she is silent. I can see myself reflected in the mirror, my daughter's face mimicking mine, and she stares at me with her large luminous eyes of the past and the future to come.

Gabi holds me and startles me from my thoughts.

"Thank you, mom," she says kissing me.

Light snow begins to fall as I drive Gabi to school. I then take the Saw Mill to the Bronx to visit my aunt Tati. Looking in my daughter's eyes today, I realized that everything is changing lately, Gabi is changing and growing and I see things in them that I had not seen before. The world is changing, and I'm changing. My change is odd and personal, a very private, womanly kind of change. I don't know my body anymore; things are moving and growing and taking a shape that wasn't mine. So I look at the woman that I am now, trying to understand the choices I've made, the causes of my sorrows or my joys, and I bless myself because a woman needs to love herself beyond the changes of time.

Tati and I catch up on family issues, *que Tío Quinto tiene problema con la próstata, y el breast cancer de la Tía Socorro* was benign. That la Tía Martirio was creating a big *chisme*, and was upset that she didn't receive an invitation to Zuki's new house.

"And Eva, have you heard from her?"

"Four boys, and still more to come. They say they bought a house in Greenwich." Tati says, *"¿Adónde es eso?"*

"Connecticut," I say. "I have to call her."

"Did you see Rica?"

"Yes," I say, and think of Rica and Estanly. Rica has four girls and Estanly has two girls outside of wedlock, looking for the boy who would carry his name. Rica still loves Estanly. They were meant for each other. He works for a local Latin radio station.

"Have you heard Estanly in the morning," Tati ask, *"Sucio."*

I laugh as Tati repeats all of Estanly's nasty jokes on the morning Latin radio station. "He's become a celebrity," she says, but this doesn't surprise me.

"Rica is going back to college, too, and she will be graduating with her Associates from Bronx Community this year," Tati says and she adds, *Y que va para* Lehman College."

"I am so proud of her," I say.

There is a silence between us and then we speak of all of the people we know who have moved on. They are spread out in California, Florida and even in Spain.

"Tati, you must come to Tarrytown."

"Hay plátanos y yuca en Tarrytown?"

"Tati, sí hay plátanos y yuca," I tell her.

Zuki and I have been trying to make Tati move to Tarrytown, but she won't. She won't live with me or with Zuki, either. I don't want to be an *estorbo* for anyone is all she says to us, and she worries about leaving the others behind in the Bronx. Tía Martirio has Mimi and Rosa, I remind her. Tati worries about Tía Socorro and others who can't afford to leave. We speak about change, about leaving the Bronx and she reminds me of cleansing the house for the New Year.

"Hay esperaté que yo te tenia la predicciones de Walter." Tati rummages inside a large white wicker basket where she kept her bills, supermarket coupons, *Vanidades* and other Latina magazines. "I had it right here," she says as she looks for the Walter Mercado's astrology magazine. Walter is an astrological guru, the Deprak Chopra in the Latino community. I'd grown up with his face on the Latino channels, his flamboyant gestures reminding me to give love, *Amor, Amor, y más Amor*.

My cousins and I would sit in front of the television to hear what was in store for us every year. He would enthusiastically urge us to take on that great job, go to school, or dump a lover that wasn't good for us, *"Dejalo, dejalo, hay más tesoros en la tierra,"* and he would do all of this as if he knew us, as if he was aware of our womanly struggles, our desires to strive and live a good life. I think back at all of the things I would do differently, but the truth is I have no regrets. Without Pito I would have no Gabi, and without Gabi I would have no Roberto.

"Ay, aqui está," she says and sits next to me to read the predictions for the upcoming prosperous year.

"*Emerges como un ave triunfadora.*"

I will emerge like a phoenix from my own ashes, she says. Success in every endeavor, particularly creative.

"This year everything transforms you, or everything falls apart, but it's all for your benefit. Accept changes like something natural, something of convenience…. You will shed skin and you will be reborn with new dreams and hopes and objectives."

"Great."

"You will be more yourself… and it will cause some people to feel envy, but no one will be able to hurt you, Ynoemia, no one because of your total faith in God."

"God is always on my side," I say in a moment of optimism.

"Listen, listen, your sign represents death, so that this is what you must do at the end of the year."

"Ok."

"*Walter dice,*" and she went on, "that in order to bring balance and peace into your life, you must go to a cemetery at the end of the year and place an offer of flowers to an abandoned grave."

"Ok," I say, and I thought of going to the cemetery in Yonkers, where there were beautiful angel statues; I had photographed them once for a project.

"*También visita una iglesia.*" I should visit a church. "With devotion," she added, looking at me sternly.

"I have devotion."

"With faith."

"I have faith."

"And take offerings of flowers and candle or something very simple like money."

"Money is not simple," I say to her, and she hushes me.

"You make love, work and money a difficult task, Ynoemia, very difficult."

I agree.

"Hear me out. Prayers, you must pray and reflect on your

life as you pray, think love, friendship, family, and money, work… it says here to think of what is out of balance in your life and bring it into balance through prayer…it's all in your hands."

"Let's see, ok," she continues, "when you pray you will let go of something you cling to from the past; in letting go of the past you will bring in the new. It's recommended here to see a healer. She may bring you guidance and the balance you are seeking."

She licks her index finger and goes on to the next page.

"Unclutter the home. Go through every room of the house and say a prayer to each room, and let go of the old, place one prayer to each room of the house. Ok. Unclutter. Let go of the past. Don't cling,"

"I don't cling."

"Mia, we all cling to some old hurt, some ancient humiliation and whenever we're down, we remember it, and don't you do that?"

"Yeah, I do."

"So, you have to let go of that old habit to bring in the new; if not, the old will stay and resentment just builds up and up, and you can't forgive, and you become just miserable and unfulfilled."

"Right."

"On New Year's Eve you must have a glass of water all night on your altar and in the morning you should throw away this water some place…the important thing is to take from that water its energy for good luck and positive vibrations."

"Ok."

"*Coge un baño de rosas,*" she says and continues in Spanish, "and dress in a wine color for the New Year. You will change this year, Ynoemia, mostly in your view of the world. No more fears. No more insecurities. No more you can't do this, you can't do that. *No más.*"

"You sound like Walter," I say and we laugh. "*No más.*"

Suddenly, Tati's words open up a door.

"*Falta más*," she says. " Walter *dice que en el último dia del año el ultimo dia.* On the last day of this year you must forgive someone who hurt you and for whom you have a hidden anger."

"*No guardes algún rencor.* I can't hold a grudge. *Este perdón tiene que ser genuino.* Your forgiveness must be genuine. Pure. Honest. It must come from your heart, Ynoemia, and she continued. "This is a powerful year for you, and there are many spiritual presences around you. Pay special attention to the people you meet. There is a lesson in every encounter."

"Ok."

"Place the Goddess Kali near your altar; she is the Hindu goddess of death. She will bring you transformation," Tía said. "Make sure you have the following rocks: Obsidian, for your sexual chakra." She stops and asks me in Spanish.

"*Adónde está el chakra sexual?*" and I show her by placing my hands on my lower abdomen.

"Ok, also have topaz, and ruby."

"*Ay*, Mia," Tía says as she comes over to me and caresses my hair. "*El mundo es espiritual*," she adds, "Cleanse your home, clear the clutter, let go of the past, and give space to the new. Don't be afraid, don't."

The following weekend when Roberto, my husband, is away on an AIDS meeting in Albany, Gabi and I begin to clean the house starting with the attic. I make a list of those I have to forgive and pray that those I have hurt forgive me. I open the creaky door of the crawl space up in the attic. Behind me, Gabi shivers.

"God it's cold in there," she says.

The attic is where I do all of my creative work, my poetry, and my collages. Sometimes when I am going to do a presentation on sexual abuse, I prepare here because it centers me, but I try to keep my trauma work at work, where I am the Program Director of a trauma center.

"I should have the attic as my bedroom, Mom," Gabi says. "I need space."

"Let me think about it," I say as we enter into the darkness of the crawl space. There are all these boxes of books and journals and dark gray garbage bags with old clothes, and the scent of old perfume and moth balls.

"God, we buy so much junk," I tell Gabi and urge her to be a good consumer.

The crawl space is a mess. Old shoes, purses and jewelry I grew bored with. Gabi's infant clothing in wicker baskets from Santo Domingo. All these wonderful foggies hidden up there: Freud, Jung, Erickson, Karen Horney, Melanie Klein, Winnicot, Thoreau, Machado, Neruda and Paz. No, these poets and psychoanalysts must come with me and be freed from these confines. I find canceled checks from my first job, my first apartment lease, my first car lease, pictures and more pictures, all in boxes, and letters from my childhood friends and my journals.

Gabi rummages around. I guide her by telling her what to move and what to put in garbage bags. Then we settle on the floor mesmerized by the memories we find. Gabi stares at me, and her eyes are bright and curious. The light enters, flickering shadows across the floor where she is sitting, and I feel this soothing comfort and love for her.

I find my past adolescence hidden in these boxes—poems, and more poems, love letters all in alphabetical order by lover and dates, more letters, and old vinyl records (woof, antiquities) the Delfonics, and other things, and then suddenly I find my father's book of prayers, and I feel a hollow feeling deep in my soul. I have to catch my breath as I hold this little book in the palm of my hand. Imprinted in the front jacket is the Sacred Heart of Jesus, *el Sagrado Corazon de Jesus*. Inside the book is a picture of my mother and father. I hold it and kiss it. I wish my parents were alive.

I find a box of old newspaper clippings from Santo Domingo when I lived there from 1972 to 1974. I collected poetry and clippings of sayings and news from the *Listín Diario* and *El Pozo de la Dicha* from another newspaper. I find my mother's jewelry and my father's favorite pen. I touch the smooth surface of the little turtle Aura gave me before she died. I find the letter she wrote me. Sometimes I wish I could speak to her and to Mami and Papi.

Then Gabi finds my Talking Board, "What's this?"

"My Ouija Board," I say and whisper, "To talk to spirits."

She whispers back, "Why are you whispering?" and we laugh.

"I guess I am whispering because I do not want to wake up the dead."

There is silence between us while I look around, just trying to figure out how to clean the house and get rid of things I no longer need, but the task is daunting. I have approximately five hundred books in the crawl space, towels, and linen I use and don't use, and I just don't know how to start to get rid of anything. I have always been like that. I have a problem with letting go.

In boxes my old journals are filed by year starting in 1972 and ending in 1999. I saved them each and then filed them. I am such a saver, a packrat. I heard that people who save things forever and ever are afraid of loss, and maybe I am. I flip through my *Libreta de los Espíritus* and read their old messages, while Gabi looks at her old boxes of Beanie babies and Spice Girls. I read through some of the journals, and I find it interesting how patterns repeat themselves, how if we look back, we can determine what errors we might make based on errors of the past.

Gabi speaks about the boys from the Bronx as she played with a box of Beanie Babies.

"They think we live upstate, and I told them this is Westchester County in New York State,"

I laugh. "I used to think this was upstate, too."

"Really?"

"Yeah, I thought Mt. Vernon was where you ski."

She laughs, "That's Vermont, Mommy."

"I later discovered that."

"I called Manuel to ask him to come to the party, and his mom is this strict Dominican mom who doesn't want him in the street or hanging out with bad kids, and she says in the background. *"Adónde es eso?'* and he says, *"En* Pennsylvania."

"Manuel, I don't live in Pennsylvania," I said to him, but by then his mother was saying, *"Tú no vas para alla carajo eso es muy lejo."*

"She sounded just like Tati," Gabi says and laughs.

She is on the floor of the crawl space with fifty of her Beanie babies which she was saving for future investment.

"I told him he should learn his geography and that we are only twenty minutes from the Bronx."

Gabi continues thanking me for letting her cousins, Eva's daughters, and the boys come to her birthday party.

"Not every mom would do what you did. That's what the boys in the Bronx said. In the Bronx, mothers are afraid of inviting the boys to their home. They think everyone is up to something bad, and so the girls, they sneak around to see the boys. The boys were surprised that you would prefer that they come over, hang out here and we could go out."

"Well, you tell the boys I'm glad they had fun and that I thought they were great. They seem to be protective of you guys, and Danny seemed so mature and organized. Francisco was nice too, but he was so intimidated, and shy. They are nice boys."

"I'm glad that you don't think the boys are hoodlums, that you respect them,"

"I'm glad that you respect my opinion, and I hope that when I sense that a boy is not good, that you will hear me out, that you will understand."

She lowers her eyes.

"Boys are just like girls," I say. "In many ways, they feel

the same way you feel so don't go around telling them bad things just because you think they don't have feelings. They do. They hurt, but they won't tell you. They feel humiliated, but they'll act tough. They feel ashamed, and they'll withdraw. They are tender boys, very tender."

"But people judge others so harshly," Gabi says. "My Dad, he doesn't want to see me on the corner anymore. He says it's dangerous, that many of the boys are drug dealers. Everyone thinks we're up to something bad. I am not that creative, yet my Dad thinks the worst, that we're up to bad things when we sit with the boys to talk in front of the building, despite the fact that Rosa and Rica are watching us from their apartment windows. Everyone thinks the boys are bad because they wear their hip hop clothing and they're shy in front of grown ups."

"Yeah, boys have it really hard, especially boys in the Bronx. You have to be soft enough to be sweet and tender to the girls you like, and then tough enough to hang out with the boys and not be called names, and it's confusing."

"Yeah," she laughs. Her eyes are shining. She looks into more boxes.

When the boys came over, I could feel their struggle. I could feel their struggle hidden behind the big tough jeans that dangled from their skinny hips, and their big jackets, and hats covering their confusion about a world they try to understand, and then try dealing with Latina girls. They want you sweet, but tough, and if you're tough, they think you're violent, but if you aren't tough, then you're not man enough.

We are silent as we move things around and Gabi finds her Beanie babies, "Can I take these downstairs? I've missed them," she says and holds onto them like when she was a young child.

She looks around in more boxes, and she finds an old red tin box from 1972, and I swallow hard when she shows it to me.

"What's this?" she asks.

"Gabi, wow, that box has little trinkets I saved from when I was thirteen. It's an old hope box. You keep things in it that remind you of hopeful things you love and cherish."

"Can I open it?"

"Sure," I say, and she does.

Inside she finds, tickets, letters, and she touches everything as if they were sacred items.

"And this?" She says and shows me an old suede cord with a whistle on it, and I think of Pito, how he carried that whistle around his neck like a trophy.

"Can I keep it?"

"Sure," I say, "but let me hold it for awhile."

Gabi passes it over and I hold onto it, and I'm transported back in time. I hold it close to me and I feel its energy, and I am back in the Bronx and I can smell Pito's musk oil, and the taste of his Juicy Fruit scent in my tongue, and I feel the warmth of that whistle he dangled on his neck like a trophy, and I feel his hands—the way the warmth of his sweaty palms touched my breast. I laugh.

Gabi's eyes shine in the darkness of the attic. She's excited about finding these memories.

"That belonged to your dad," I say, and she's awed by the presence of the whistle as if she's found an ancient artifact, and she presses her warm lips against the old whistle, blows on it, and it sings.

Acknowledgments

This book reflects a healing journey that began a long time ago. I have had important guides, mentors, spirits and helpers all of whom I thank for their unending support.

I want to thank my husband, David, whose unconditional love provides the foundation for creative work to flow, and my daughter, Annelise, who has been a joy and inspiration. Boundless gratitude and praise to Sandy Taylor, at Curbstone Press, whose vision and mission made this possible and to Benjamin A. Saenz, whose work I so admired, and who selected my manuscript for publication.

Gracias to my sister, Mary Crespo, who has been more like a mother than a sister, and to Maria Crespo who has helped me out in times of need without complaint or expectations; to Cristina Uribe de Baez who has been a blessed stepmother and whose wisdom and compassion I so admire.

Thanks also go to my family and friends who have been there in times of need and in times of joy, and whose faith in me has always been constant. Thank you Michael Thomas, who read these stories in their tender beginnings and whose nurturing editorial suggestions allowed the stories to grow; and to my literary friends, Nelly Rosario, Angie Cruz, Sophie Marinez, and Marianela Medrano, whose conversations about life, love and the writing life have sustained me.

Thank you to Ruth Herrera who translated The Red Shoes and it appeared as "Tacones Altos", in Caudal, 11/04, in the Dominican Republic, gracias Carlos Cabrera. "The Silence of Angels" first appeared in Callaloo 23.3, Summer 2000 and "Amor Sucks" appeared in Latinarte. Thank you!

The term "Casarte" was first used by Josefina Baez as a term to describe her performance theatre in a house or apartment. Thank you Josefina for letting me use this term as the inspiration for this story.

To a great mentor and friend, Silvio Torres-Saillant whose support and encouragement gave me the faith needed to keep on writing despite multiple roles and to las Tertuliantes, thank you Daisy Cocco De Filippis, for providing a safe space for Latina women to share their process, their stories and their lives.

I also want to thank those amazing individuals I have met at Lehman College, you know who you are. Particular thanks go to the young women who surround me with their stories of strength and the young men whose determination to beat the odds is a true inspiration. Thank you all.

Finally, thank you God for the blessings and inspirations and to my living elders whose wisdom lights my path and to those who have departed, I miss your presence here on earth, but find comfort in your loving memory and silent guidance.